D0897721

For Reference

Not to be taken from this room

Celebrate the World

Celebrate
the World

Twenty Tellable Folktales
for Multicultural Festivals

by Margaret Read MacDonald

Illustrations by Roxane Murphy Smith

The H.W. Wilson Company
1994

Dedicated to James Bruce MacDonald,
who introduced me to the Highland Games and
gave me two little girls to dance the Fling!

Printed in the United States of America
First Printing

CONTENTS

CONTENTS

CONTENTS

ACKNOWLEDGMENTS

My gratitude to all of these folks for advice in the preparation of this book: Mariko Martin, Robin and Bryan Yim, Oline Heath, The Islamic School of Seattle, Parveen Zadeh, Jorge and Mary Garcia, Valerie Dillon, Jane Weiss and members of the How's Bayou Cajun Band, Anjali Kumar and Radhika Kumar, Michel Roqui, Christine Harmel of Dijon, and Jennifer MacDonald.

Thanks to Judy O'Malley for careful editing and such enthusiastic encouragement that I can't wait to show her my next story.

INTRODUCTION

These tales were selected because they are fun to tell. They are set in a readable ethnopoetic format which makes them easy to learn, and I have added notes for each tale to help you perform them. I hope you will fall in love with several of these stories and tell them on many occasions, not just on the days of special celebrations. For several years I have been setting aside stories from my repertoire which I thought might be fun to use for festive programs. And in recent years I have tried these out within the context of special library programs celebrating the world's holidays. In this collection I suggest these stories as an ingredient for holiday celebrations in the classroom or the library. To help you in your program planning I include bibliographies for further reading about these holidays, suggested books to share with children during these celebrations, and a handful of activities for each. I have asked a friend from each of these cultures to look over my programs and make suggestions. I hope I am doing justice to the many pleasures that each ethnic group enjoys as it celebrates.

TO PRODUCE A SUCCESSFUL CELEBRATION

1. Decorate your space in appropriate festive colors and arrange a display of objects relating to the holiday.
2. Share a picture book from the list of suggested "Books to Share," talk about the festival, and show pictures of the festive celebration taking place.
3. Tell the story from this book.
4. Play a game or carry out a dramatic activity related to your theme.
5. Create a festive craft to take home.
6. Listen to music traditional to this celebration. This can be a special activity, or you can play the music as the children arrive and during their craft and food period.
7. Snack on traditional foods.

To make your own celebrations as rich as possible try to discover someone from the culture you are celebrating to help you produce the event. Many people are delighted to share if you just ask.

If using story in multicultural celebrations pleases you, you might also enjoy a collection of tales from Jewish holidays by Nina Jaffe, *The Uninvited Guest and Other Jewish Holiday Tales,* illustrated by Elivia Savadier (New York: Scholastic, Inc., 1993). For tales to accompany eleven feasts from India, see *Seasons of Splendour: Tales, Myths, and Legends of India* by Madhur Jaffrey (New York: Atheneum, 1985). *Tales of a Chinese Grandmother* by Frances Carpenter (Garden City, N.Y.: Doubleday, Doran & Co., 1937) and *Tales from a Taiwan Kitchen* by Cora Cheny (New York: Dodd, Mead, 1976) also contain stories for several holidays.

ABOUT THESE TALES

I provide source notes for these stories so you can track down the originals from which I worked if you like, and my notes will help you think too about the many other variants of these tales. I take playful liberties with some of the stories, and two of the tales, "Escargot On His Way to Dijon" and "Forget-Me-Not," were re-created from very brief fragments into lengthy stories. In some cases, "Benizara and Kakezara" for example, I combine elements from two stories to create my new version. All of this is explained in the tale notes.

Beginning tellers might want to start with "Little Rooster and the Heavenly Dragon," the story of a dragon who steals the rooster's horns, with "Forget-Me-Not," a legend exlaining how this tiny flower got it's name, or with "Nail Soup," a slurping version of an old favorite which I learned from Oline Heath, a Norwegian-American friend whom I met at an elderhostel. Another easy-to-tell tale is "The Silver Pine Cones," the tale of a poor woman who encounters the Dwarf King in the forest. He chants a fearful "BY MY BOOTS AND BY MY BEARD, WHO'S STEALING MY PINE CONES?" but then turns kindly.

Those who enjoy rollicking audience-participation will have great fun with "Poule and Roach," the tale of a cockroach who marries a hen and then parties with his cockroach buddies all day while the hen (Poule) works. Lots of drumming and singing in this one! Great fun also is "Papa God and the Pintards", a singing and dancing tale about birds whose singing gets even God tapping his toes. And "Going to Cervières" with it's repeated chant as Goose and his friends climb to Cervières for their health after a Christmas sweets binge, will delight any audience-participation fan.

Two tales with delightful group participation *sound effects* are "Escargot On His Way to Dijon," the French tale of a snail who slides all the way to Dijon, beating the wolf to the cathedral for Easter Mass, and "Little Snot Nose Boy," the Japanese story of a snot-nosed child who creates gold just by blowing his nose! You can *imagine* the sound effects on *this* one!

Two somewhat quieter stories are "The Clever Daughter-in-Law," the Chinese story of a young girl who solves the riddle of bringing fire and wind wrapped in paper, and "Todo o Nada," the tale of a man who discovers a treasure cave . . . only to be told he must take all or nothing at all.

More difficult to learn, but well worth the effort, is the Japanese Cinderella variant "Benizara and Kakezara." Children find this tale magical. They are pleased also by two male Cinderella twists: "The Finger Lock," a Scottish tale in which a wee man gives a bagpipe and a magic tune to a lad, and "Yao Jour," the Hmong tale of a young man who is latched onto at the dance by *two* girls. Another difficult, but worth-the-effort tale, is "The Small Yellow Dragon." Your audience will excitedly toss dumplings into the water to nourish the small Chinese Dragon as he fights his large Black Dragon enemy.

Some stories *appear* lengthy but will be easy to tell. "Stinky Spirits" is the story of a kind boy who treats with respect the foul-smelling spirits who inhabit his yam field at night. His unkind stepbrother mocks them—with dire results. "Sparrow Song" tells of a little sparrow who tricks passersby out of their goods until he has the ingredients for his rice pudding. "The Pumpkin Child" is a magical tale of a pumpkin child and the beautiful girl who emerges from that pumpkin when the prince is watching. All three of these tales have delightful chants which will make their delivery easier. "Sparrow Song" and "The Pumpkin Child" can involve the audience in their chants.

Lastly I will mention two more easy-to-learn tales. "The Old Woman in a Pumpkin Shell" is an Iranian version of a popular folk motif in which an old woman or small animal rolls along in a pumpkin or drum tricking ferocious animals on the way home. This story can be told alone, or in conjunction with "The Pumpkin Child." Perhaps my favorite tale of all is "Sparrow and His Wife," an Iraqi tale of a husband who angers his wife and chants plaintively at her nest every day until it occurs to him to bring her five bright threads . . . which win her back!

As you can see, this book is a treasury of fun-to-tell stories for *any* day of the year. Have fun playing with them during your holiday celebrations, but keep telling them *all year long!*

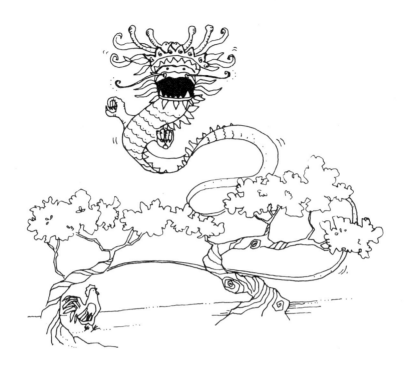

THE LITTLE ROOSTER AND
THE HEAVENLY DRAGON

A folktale from China.

In days long ago the Rooster had beautiful golden horns.
Every morning he would strut up and down in the yard calling
        "LOOK at my golden HORNS!
        LOOK at my golden HORNS!"
He was so proud of those horns.

One day as the Rooster was crowing,
the magnificent Heavenly Dragon came soaring down from the skies.

      "Little Rooster, you have such *beautiful* golden horns!"

"Aren't they marvelous?
I have the finest horns in the universe!"

"Little Rooster, I would like to ask you a favor.
I have been invited to a banquet at the Jade Emperor's
    palace in heaven tonight.
If I could wear your golden horns,
I would be the most magnificent creature there.
Do you think I could borrow yours horns?
Just for one night?"

"I don't think so.
I *never* lend my horns to *anyone*."

"But Little Rooster you can trust ME.
I am the magnificent Heavenly Dragon!"

"How do I know you will bring them back?
You might just stay up in heaven and never return."

"If you aren't sure you can trust me,
why not ask my cousin the Centipede.
He is your neighbor.
He lives right here in the farmyard.
You can trust *his word*."

So Little Rooster called his neighbor, the Centipede.
    "Centipede! Centipede!
    Come over here and talk to me."

Centipede began to wriggle his one hundred legs.

He came out from his hiding place and wobbled over to see what
Rooster wanted.

"Centipede is this Dragon really your cousin?"

Centipede looked at the Dragon.
Dragon was glaring at Centipede.
Dragon looked VERY dangerous.
"Say YES," he hissed.

"Yes," whispered the little centipede.

"Can I trust him to bring back my horns?"

"Say YES," hissed the Dragon.

"Yes," whispered Centipede.

"Since you are my neighbor,
I trust you little Centipede.
All right, Dragon.
I will lend you my horns.
But bring them back FIRST THING tomorrow morning."

The Rooster removed his golden horns.
He placed them on the head of the Dragon.

OFF flew the Dragon!
"Now *I* am the most magnificent creature in the universe!

SEE-E-E-E my GOLDEN HORNS!
SEE-E-E-E my GOLDEN HORNS!"

Dragon tossed his head proudly and flew back and forth through the air, showing off.

That evening, the Dragon wore the horns to the banquet at the Jade Emperor's palace in heaven.

How everyone did admire those golden horns.

The Dragon was so proud of his new adornments.

"Such horns belong on the head of a magnificent creature like myself . . . not on a puny little rooster!"

Next morning the Rooster was up early watching the skies.

He was waiting for the Dragon to return his horns.

"Bring back my HORNS!" he called to the skies.

"Bring back my HORNS!"

But the Dragon did not return.

He did not return that morning.

He did not return the next.

He NEVER returned.

To this day the Heavenly Dragon still wears those *beautiful* golden horns.

The Rooster was SO angry.

He called up the little Centipede.

"Centipede, you told me the Dragon would bring back my horns!

You lied to me!"

Rooster was so angry, he PECKED at Centipede and ate him up.

To this day, everytime Rooster sees a Centipede he PECKS at it and eats it up.

4

And every morning Rooster looks up to the skies and calls
"Bring back my HORNS!
Bring back my HORNS!
Bring back my HORNS!"

But the Heavenly Dragon never brings them back.

NOTES ON TELLING

When Rooster calls to the skies, his words should echo a crowing sound. "LOOK at my Golden HORNS!" and "BRING back my HORNS!"

Make much of the Dragon's flight through the sky showing off his golden horns "See-e-e-e my Golden Horns!" and tossing his head proudly.

This story works well as tandem telling, story theater, or as a simple puppet play.

The "Jade Emperor" is ruler of heaven, surrounded by a pantheon of gods. To be invited to his banquet table is the highest honor.

The centipede is one of the "five poisonous insects" which are exterminated on the 5th day of the 5th month. The cock is the centipede's primary enemy. Use this story for your Double Fifth program (see p. 101) as well as here. Leslie Bonnet's version of this story uses an earthworm for Cock's barnyard enemy and I have always told this story using an earthworm. "Little Earthworm! Little Earthworm! Come out of the ground and talk to me!" says my Rooster. However in researching for the tale notes I discovered that Wolfram Eberhard's original text speaks of a "millipede" and specifically notes the association with Double Fifth. Since most sources describe the five poisonous insects as including a "centipede," I have used that insect for this version. See my notes for the Double Fifth celebration for more information about the "five poisounous insects" tradition.

COMPARATIVE NOTES

This tale is elaborated from a variant in Leslie Bonnet's, *Chinese Folk and Fairy Tales* (New York: Putnam, 1958), pp. 111–114. Bonnet's version is based on Wolfram Eberhard's version in *Folktales of China* (Chicago: University of Chicago Press, 1965), pp. 5–6, "Why Does the Cock Eat the Millipede?" Other variants appear in Roger Lancelyn Green's *A Cavalcade of Dragons* (New York: Walck,

1972), pp. 157–160 and in a picture book by Ed Young, with Hilary Beckett, *The Rooster's Horns* (New York: Collins and World, 1978).

For tales of other animals borrowing and not returning see Margaret Read MacDonald's *The Storyteller's Sourcebook* A2241 *Animal characteristics: borrowing and not returning*. This source cites a Mayan tale in which a turkey borrows a whipporwill's feathers to wear to the king's election, a Japanese tale in which a cricket borrows an earthworm's voice, and a Russian tale in which a wagtail borrows a wren's tail to wear to a wedding. Stith Thompson's *Motif-Index of Folk-Literature* cites variants of A2241 from India, Finland, Japan, Rhodesia, Ekoi, and Menomini sources. *The Types of the Folktale* by Antti Aarne and Stith Thompson lists Finnish, Irish, French, Catalan, German, Polish, and Puerto Rican variants under Type 234 *The Nightingale and the Blindworm*. Each has one eye. The nightingale borrows the blindworm's eye and then refuses to return it. Since then, she has two eyes, the blindworm none. The latter is always on a tree where a nightingale has her nest and in revenge bores holes in the nightingale's eggs. Reference to this tale appears also in Shakespeare's *Romeo and Juliet,* Act III, line 31. Type 235 *The Jay Borrows the Cuckoo's Skin and Fails to Return It* is found in Finland, Lithuania, Ireland, Germany, Russia, and Indonesia.

NEW YEAR IN THE CHINESE TRADITION

The New Year officially begins with the first new moon after the sun enters Aquarius. This can occur between January 21 and February 9. Families gather to dine on special dishes on New Year's Eve and the head of the family pays respect to the family's ancestors. At midnight the din of firecrackers being set off all over town raises such a ruckus that all evil spirits are frightened away. On New Year's Day families begin visits to friends and relatives. Piles of round, golden oranges or tangerines symbolizing wealth and good luck are found in every house and are carried as gifts. Children are presented with red paper packets embossed with gold good luck symbols and containing small gifts of money. Above each door a good luck symbol painted in gold on red paper invites good luck for the coming year. To celebrate the holiday, martial arts groups may roam the streets performing lion dances and collecting money for charity. A New Year's parade may be held featuring a dragon dance, exciting drumming, and more firecrackers! The New Year season extends until Moon 1, Day 15. In many areas the fifteenth day is celebrated with a Lantern Festival. Children parade carrying paper lanterns. Or the festival may include more dragon dancing, fireworks, and feasting. The New Year traditions vary throughout China and in the many overseas Chinese communities.

SUGGESTIONS FOR A NEW YEAR CELEBRATION

Tell: "The Little Rooster and the Heavenly Dragon"
  or "The Small Yellow Dragon" (pp. 89–99)
  or "The Clever Daughter-in-Law" (pp. 137–145)

Decorate the room with good luck symbols traced in gold on red paper. Most books about Chinese New Year will show these.

Practice the Chinese words for "Happy New Year," "Gung Hay Fat Choy" and show the characters for these words in Chinese (below).

Prepare a pile of tangerines or oranges to admire. Eat them during your celebration.

Talk about the Chinese zodiac. Let each child find out which horoscope sign they were born under.

Expand your storytime with tales about the animal honored in this year . . . i.e. The Year of the Monkey, The Year of the Rat, etc.

Pass out red paper packets. You can purchase these in Chinese gift shops, or you could fold them from bright red paper. King County librarian, Joyce Wagar, asks

the children to give their birth year when they sign up for her program. She locates a penny minted in the year of each child's birth and presents this to the child in the red paper packet. Note however that the gift of a single small coin could be considered bad luck in Chinese tradition.

Make a paper dragon puppet.

See also: Double Fifth, p. 101; Mid-Autumn Feast, p. 146.

TO LEARN MORE ABOUT THIS HOLIDAY

See entries for China, Hong Kong, Mauritius, Taiwan, and People's Republic of China under "Moon l, Days 1–15: The New Year" in *Folklore of World Holidays* by Margaret Read MacDonald (Detroit: Gale Research, 1992).

Chinese Festivals in Hong Kong by Joan Law and Barbara E. Ward (Hong Kong: South China Morning Post, 1982.) Color photos and fascinating comments.

Chinese New Year: Fact and Folklore by William C. Hu (Ann Arbor, Michigan: Ars Ceramica, 1991). Four hundred pages of information, including recipes.

Fun with Chinese Festivals by Tan Huay Peng. Illus. by Leon Kum Chuen (Union City, Calif.: Heian International, Inc., 1991). Humorous and informative publication prepared by two Singapore cartoonists.

BOOKS TO SHARE WITH CHILDREN

Chin Chiang and the Dragon's Dance by Ian Wallace. Illus. by author (New York: Atheneum, 1984). Set in Vancouver, British Columbia's Chinatown. A young boy lacks the confidence to carry the dragon's tail in the New Year parade. An old woman janitress gives him the courage to dance. The book has been criticized for implying that the old woman could take his role in the dragon dance, apparently an inaccurate plot line.

"The God That Lived in the Kitchen," "Guardians of the Gate," "The Painted Eyebrow," and "Ting Tan and the Lamb" in *Tales of a Chinese Grandmother* by Frances Carpenter (Garden City, New York: Doubleday, Doran & Co., 1937).

The Chinese New Year by Cheng Hou-tien. (New York: Holt, Rinehart and Winston, 1976). Descriptions of "The Little New Year" . . . a time of preparation; "The

Five Days of Chinese New Year"; and "The Lantern Festival" . . . a feast of the first full moon which concludes the New Year season. Illustrated in papercuts by the author. Includes the Chinese zodiac. (New York: Holt, Rinehart & Winston, 1976).

Chinese New Year by Tricia Brown, photographs by Fran Ortiz. (New York: Henry Holt and Co., 1987). Black and white photographs and clear text show a Chinese family in San Francisco preparing for New Year and celebrating.

Lion Dancer: Ernie Wan's Chinese New Year by Kate Waters and Madeline Slovenz-Low. Photographs by Martha Cooper. (New York: Scholastic, 1990). New Year's Eve and New Year's Day with Ernie Wan, his family, and his father's Kung Fu school in New York City. His father's school performs Lion Dances for the New Year Parade and Ernie and his little sister have been trained to dance with their own smaller lion. An excellent book to share the excitement of children at New Year with your class.

PICTURE BOOKS ABOUT THE ZODIAC

The Rat, the Ox, and the Zodiac: A Chinese Legend by Dorothy Van Woerkom. Illus. by Errol Le Cain (New York: Crown, 1976).

Why Rat Comes First: The Story of the Chinese Zodiac by Clara Yen (San Francisco: Children's Book Press, 1991).

BENIZARA AND KAKEZARA

A folktale from Japan.

There once was a girl named Benizara.

Benizara means "crimson plate."

Benizara lived with her stepmother and a stepsister named Kakezara.

Kakezara means "broken plate" and the two girls were much like
    their names.

As so often happens in these old tales, Benizara's stepmother treated
    her poorly.

Benizara was made to do all of the work around the house, and she
    was given only old clothes to wear.

Kakezara was given every beautiful thing she wanted.

She spent her days trying on beautiful kimonos, fixing her hair with expensive ornaments, and powdering her face.

She would look in the mirror all day long,

> "Aren't I BEAUTIFUL?
>
> Thank goodness I don't look like that ugly Benizara in her ragged old clothes."

The stepmother arranged for Kakezara to be taught all the things a young lady should know.

Kakezara was given music lessons and learned to play the samisen.

Kakezara was given calligraphy lessons and shown how to use the writing brush.

Kakezara was given books of poetry and taught how to compose haiku.

But Kakezara did not care for any of these things.

She did her lessons halfheartedly and hurried back to her mirror.

Poor Benizara wanted so badly to learn to play a musical instrument.

She would have loved to have books of poetry to read, or brushes and paper to write with.

But she was given nothing but dust rags and brooms.

One day the stepmother called Benizara and Kakezara and gave them each a bag for gathering chestnuts.

> "Go into the forest and gather a few chestnuts for us today."

To Kakezara she gave a small, tightly woven bag.

To Benizara she gave a large bag. It was very old and rotting away so that it was full of holes.

When the girls reached the forest Kakezara quickly filled her bag.

But Benizara could not make a single chestnut stay in her bag.

Everytime she dropped one in, it fell right out at the bottom.

If she held the bottom together, the chestnut fell out at the side.
Kakezara picked up her tiny bag and turned to go home.

> "Wait, don't leave Kakezara.
> I don't want to stay alone in the forest."
> "Then you should have worked harder and filled your bag
>   like *I* did."

Kakezara turned her back and walked away.

Benizara worked even harder now.
She was frightened to remain alone in the forest.
But it was hopeless.
There was no way to carry chestnuts in that rotten bag.

Then she heard a rustling in the bushes.
> "What is it? A bear?"

But when she looked up she saw a little white dove.
The dove cocked it's head and looked at her.
> "I know who you are.
> You are Benizara.
> Here, let me help you."

The dove picked grass from the ground and began to weave it into
    Benizara's bag.
The dove wove a bit here . . . she wove a bit there . . .
soon she had repaired all of the holes in the bag.
Then the dove helped Benizara pick up chestnuts and drop them in,
    until the bag was full.
> "Now you can go home and your stepmother will not be
>   angry with you.
> But I have something to show you first.
> Follow me."

The dove led the way into a little clearing.

There lay a large box.
        "Open it!
        Open it!"
Benizara lifted the lid of the box.
Inside was a beautiful silk kimono.
She held it up.
It was just her size!
She tried it on.
It fit perfectly.
With the kimono was a lovely obi with it's big bow.
She fastened the obi around her waist.
And there were elegant ornaments for her hair too!

        "Is all this for ME?"

        "This is for YOU.
        Take the box home.
        But do not show it to your stepmother.
        She would take it away and give it to Kakezara.

        And I have something else for you Benizara."

The little dove held something in her beak.
Benizara took it gently.
It was a tiny flute made of a hollyhock stem.

        "It is small, but it will make wonderful music," said the
        Dove.

Benizara tucked the hollyhock flute into her sleeve.
She hurried home with her bag of chestnuts and the box.

13

Benizara hid the box behind the house, then she went into the house with her chestnuts.

"You are home so soon?"

The stepmother had hoped Benizara might get lost and stay in the forest.

"Well, give me your bag and get back to work."

Every day after that, Benizara would tiptoe out and take a peek at her beautiful kimono. But she never dared put it on for fear her stepmother would discover it.

But she DID bring out the hollyhock flute and play it.

She practiced and practiced and what beautiful music she learned to make!

The next week was the village festival.

The stepmother dressed Kakezara in her most beautiful kimono.

"The Daimyo's son will be at the festival.

Perhaps he will notice my beautiful daughter!"

To Benizara the stepmother said,

"Clean the floor, dust the windows, and dust the rafters.

Scrub the kitchen pots, wash the clothes, and weed the garden. When you are finished you may come to the festival."

This work would take the entire day.

Benizara knew she would never get to the festival.

While she was cleaning, the neighborhood girls came by in their beautiful kimonos.

"Benizara, aren't you coming to the festival?"

"I can't go. Stepmother said I had to clean the entire house before I could leave."

"What a pity.

But WE could help you!"

14

One girl began to dust the rafters.

Another began to clean the windows.

A third swept the floor.

A fourth weeded the garden.

A fifth washed the clothes.

And Benizara scrubbed the pots.

In no time all of the tasks were finished.

"Now come with us, Benizara!"

"Wait until I change my clothes."

"But that is the only kimono you have."

"No it isn't. Just wait!"

Benizara went behind the house and opened her box.

She put on the beautiful silk kimono.

She put on the lovely obi.

Her girlfriends helped her put up her hair and fix the elegant hair
ornaments.

"Ohhhh you are so BEAUTIFUL!

You look like a LADY!

We didn't know you were so BEAUTIFUL Benizara."

The girls hurried to the festival.

Everywhere there were exciting things to see.

They watched the dancers.

They watched the puppet show.

They stopped to watch a man who was making dolls dance.

One of Benizara's friends bought a bag of *ame* sweets and gave two
to Benizara.

Benizara took off the wrapper and ate one.

Then she saw Kakezara and her stepmother in the crowd.

Kakezara was tugging at her mother's sleeve.

"Mother, Mother, buy me some *AME*.

15

Buy me some *AME*."

"I can share," thought Benizara.

She wadded up the candy wrapper and threw it at Kakezara.

The candy wrapper hit Kakezara in the cheek.

When Kakezara turned to look, Benizara tossed her the second candy.

"Here. I'll share with you."

Kakezara ate the candy.

Then she tugged on her mother's sleeve.

"Mother! Mother!

Benizara threw an *ame* wrapper and hit me in the face!"

"Don't be foolish.

Benizara is at home cleaning the house."

Benizara's friend bought some *dango* sweets and gave two to
Benizara.

Benizara ate one.

Then she saw Kakezara tugging at her mother's sleeve again.

"Mother, Mother, buy me *DANGO*."

"I can share." thought Benizara.

She wadded up the *dango* wrapper and threw it at Kakezara.

The dango wrapper hit Kakezara in the cheek.

When Kakezara turned she whispered.

"Here . . . catch!" and tossed her a *dango*.

Kakezara took off the wrapper and ate the *dango*.

Then she tugged on her mother's sleeve again.

"Mother! Mother! Benizara threw a *dango* wrapper and hit
me in the face!"

"Don't be foolish. Benizara is at home cleaning.

If someone throws something at you just turn the other way
and ignore them."

16

Now the son of the Daimyo WAS in the crowd that day.
He had noticed Benizara.
> "What a beautiful young girl.
> How lovely she looks in that kimono."
His heart began to beat faster.

And when he saw her sharing her candies with her sister he realized
  that she was not only beautiful but good hearted as well.
He sent a servant to follow her and discover where she lived.

When Benizara returned home she changed back into her old clothes
  and returned to her cleaning.
That evening there was a knocking at the door.
There stood the Daimyo's son and his servants.
> "I believe you have a beautiful young lady living here.
> I would like to get to know her better."
> "Yes! Yes!
> Kakezara come quickly!"
But when the Daimyo's son saw Kakezara his face fell.
> "You must have *another* young lady in this household."
> "No. No one except grubby little Benizara there."
The Daimyo's son looked at Benizara.
He thought he recognized that face.
But the *clothing* was so ragged.
> "I would like to get to know these two girls better.
> Perhaps they could entertain me."
The Daimyo's son sat down and waited.
> "Quick, Kakezara bring out the samisen and play for the
>   young lord."
Kakezara brought out her samisen.
She had never liked to practice at this instrument.
And she HATED to perform.

17

With a frown she sat down.

> "Plunk . . . plunk . . . TWANG!
> Plunk . . . plunk . . . TWANG!"

What an unpleasant sound she made.

The Daimyo's son listened politely.

> "Now, will the second daughter entertain me?"

Benizara took out her little hollyhock flute.

She began to play.

Such sweet music.

The prince was enthralled.

> "Now, perhaps the girls would compose a poem for me.
> Let me give them a subject for their poem."

The prince placed a tray on the table.

On the tray he placed a plate.

On the plate he placed a pile of white salt.

Into the mound of salt, he stuck a pine needle.

> "Now. Compose a poem."

Kakezara stared.

How she hated poetry.

But she had to try.

> "There is a tray on the table.
> There is a plate on the tray.
> And a pile of salt.
> And a pine needle.
> It's going to fall over in a minute.
> There! A poem!"

The Daimyo's son shook his head.

> "What a poor poem, she just named what she saw."

Benizara knew that a poem must be thoughtful and carry beauty.

She began.

> "A wide plain.
> From the plain a snowy mountain rises.
> On the mountain a lone pine tree
> Grows . . . and grows."

> "Ahhh. What a lovely image.
> A FINE poem.
> THIS is the young lady I would like to get to know better.
> May she accompany me to the palace?"

> "Wait," said Benizara.
> "I must change my clothes."
> "But that's the only kimono you have," said her stepmother.

Benizara ran behind the house.
She put on the beautiful silk kimono.
She put on the lovely obi sash.
She fixed up her hair and put in the elegant ornaments.
When she returned everyone gasped.

> "YES! THIS is the young lady I saw at the festival!
> YOU will come with ME!"

So Benizara was whisked away to the palace.
And when the Daimyo's son got to know her better he liked her very
  much and you can guess what happened . . .
they were married and lived happily every after!
The END.

NOTES ON TELLING

Take time with your telling as Benizara dresses herself. Put on your imagined
kimono, obi, and hair ornaments slowly, so the children can envision her pleasure

19

with these lovely items. If the Japanese kimono and obi are not familiar to your children you may want to show pictures or display a Japanese doll in kimono before you tell the story.

You might also want to share a few haiku before you begin the story, so that the children have some sense of the sort of poem Benizara is expected to create. In the classroom setting the introduction of a cultural background for the story could take place earlier in the week, before the story is shared, rather than as a preface to the tale itself.

COMPARATIVE NOTES

This is a variant of the Cinderella story, Type 510. Thirty-six variants from twenty-five cultures are cited in MacDonald's *The Storyteller's Sourcebook* under R221 *Heroine's threefold flight from the ball*. Ceylonese, Chinese, Korean, and Vietnamese variants are listed, but none resembles this tale with its trip to the festival and its poetry contest. In the "gift of clothing from a dove," "home visit by a prince to seek out a lost bride," and "wicked stepmother and stepsister" we see direct relationship to other Cinderella tales, however.

A variant of this Japanese tale is found in *Folktales of Japan* by Robert J. Adams (p. 130–134). That variant is titled "Benizara and Kakezara," however the tale is listed in Japanese folklore studies as Kata No. 210 *Komebuku and Awabuku* and as Kata No. 211 *Dish Dish Mountain*. Over thirty-seven versions of the tale have been recorded in Japan. Adams tells us that red is a felicitous color in Japan, hence the value of "Crimson dish" as a name. The version given in *Folktales of Japan* was collected in Hamatsu City, Skizuoka-Ken by Hana Watanabe. The actual poem given is in the Waka or Tanka poetic form, with a 5–7–5–7–7 syllable arrangement. It is:

Bon zara ya	Tray, plate, oh!
sara chuu yami ni	plate on mountain over
yuki furite	snow falls
yuki o ne toshite	snow as root using
sodatsu matsu ka na.	growing pine it seems.

Adams translates the two girls' poems as:
    Put a plate on a tray,
    Put some salt on the plate,

Stick a pine needle in the salt;
It'll soon fall over.

A tray and plate, oh!
A mountain rises from the plate,
On it, snow has fallen.
Rooted deep into the snow,
A lonely pine tree grows.

The Adams' version of the story is related also to Q2.2 *Kind and Unkind Girls* (Type 480). Benizara is taken in by an old woman spinning who says her two ogre sons will soon be coming. Benizara is given a magic box which will provide for her if she taps it three times. She is to spread rice around her mouth and lie down as if dead if she encounters the oni sons. She obeys and they leave her alone, assuming maggots are coming out of her mouth. Later the magic box provides a kimono which she wears to a play where she throws the candies and is seen by the nobleman.

A second version of this story "Nukabuku, Komebuku" is found in *Ancient Tales in Modern Japan: An Anthology of Japanese Folk Tales* by Fanny Hagin Mayer (p.44–46). In this version a "beautiful white bird" tells Komebukuro that she was the girl's mother in her former life. She provides a dress, a new bag to gather chestnuts, and a hollyhock flute. Komebukuru walks to the festival playing her hollyhock flute, which sings:

Whoever hears this little flute—
Birds in flight across the sky,
Rest your wings and listen;
Worms that crawl upon the ground,
Halt your feet and listen.

Komebukuro stops at the shrine where her sister and mother are "watching dolls dance" and throws the *dango* wrapper. Instead of the poetry contest this tale has a scene in which the girls fix their hair and the stepmother tells Komebukuro to put water from the kitchen drain on hers rather than the oil she gives her own daughter. Wanting her own daughter to ride in a sedan chair, she puts her into a cart and hauls her off. The cart overturns into a rice paddy and the daughter turns into a mudsnail. The mother falls into the mill pond and turns into a sluice shellfish. This version was collected from Kawai Yutaro, Tsugaru, Aomori. A related tale called "Sara-Sara Yama" is also given in Fanny Hagin Meyer's collection. It includes the poetry episode.

GIRL'S DAY: HINA MATSURI

A Japanese tradition.

In Japan the third day of the third month is traditionally a celebration for young girls. This is celebrated today on March 3. Each girl sets up an elaborate display of special dolls in her home. Steps are arranged against a wall, from three to seven steps depending on the grandeur of the doll display. The steps are covered with a red cloth and the dolls are arranged on the steps. The Lord and Lady dolls, often called Emperor and Empress, hold court on the highest step, with the rest of their entourage set out below. The display may include samurai, ladies playing samisen, musicians, and other courtiers. The young girls of the household may invite friends for this day. All dine on special treats and tea as they sit before the doll display admiring it. The dolls displayed on this day are generally family heirlooms and must be stored carefully away in their boxes by the next day. According to some customs, the girl who fails to put her doll display away properly may never marry!

SUGGESTIONS FOR A CELEBRATION OF HINA MATSURI

Arrange your own doll display. Arrange a tier covered with red cloth to display the dolls. If possible, ask a Japanese friend to loan her doll display for the day. If there are no Japanese friends in your community, let children bring their own special dolls from home for your display. Or create a display of origami dolls to fill your shelves.

Drink Japanese tea and eat sweet rice cakes or cookies as you sit before your doll display and admire it.

Listen to a recording of Japanese samisen or traditional court music.

Ask a Japanese friend to talk about Hina Matsuri celebrations when she was a child.

Make origami empress and emperor dolls: Make two simple origami dolls. Paste them sitting upright on a piece of origami paper. Pleat a fourth piece of origami paper and paste it at their backs as a backdrop screen. Patterns for a very simple doll or for an elaborate display of fifteen origami dolls are found in *Matsuri Festival* by Nancy K. Araki & Jane M. Horii (Union City, Ca.: Heian International, Inc., 1978), p. 62–77. Patterns for a more complicated set of male and female dolls are found in *Origami: The Art of Paperfolding* by Robert Harbin (New York: Harper & Row, 1969), p. 156–163.

FOR MORE INFORMATION ON HINA MATSURI

"Dolls' Day and Boys' Day" in *Festivals in Asia.*
Sponsored by the Asian Cultural Centre for Unesco. (Tokyo: Kodansha, 1975), p. 23–30.

"Girl's Day" in *Folklore of American Holidays* by Tristram Potter Coffin and Hennig Cohen (Detroit: Gale Research, 1991), p. 105.

"Hina Matsuri" in *Folklore of World Holidays* by Margaret Read MacDonald (Detroit: Gale Research, 1992), p. 156–158.

"Hinamatsuri" in *Matsuri: Festival. Japanese American Celebrations and Activities* by Nancy K. Araki and Jane M. Horii (Union City, Ca.: Heian International Inc., 1978), p. 54–77.
Best source. Gives detailed history of holiday.

The out-of-print children's novel *Suzu and the Bride Doll* by Patricia Miles Martin (Chicago: Rand McNally, 1960) contains a detailed description of a Doll's Day celebration as does *Noriko: Girl of Japan* by Dominique Darbois (Chicago: Follett, 1964), also out of print.

TODO O NADA

A story from Brownsville, Texas.

Down in Brownsville, Texas, there's gold buried in the hills, so they
   say.

Up the Rio Grande River lies a little town called Santa Cruz,
There was a poor farmer there, Cesario Balderas was his name.
The time was 1875.
There is always talk of gold treasure hidden in the hills.
Gold left by the Spaniards.
Gold buried by pirates.
Even gold hidden in recent times by bootleggers on the run from the
   Texas Rangers.

But no one has actually *found* hidden treasure.

Except for . . .

One day, the cow of Cesario Balderas ran away.

He hunted up the ravines, climbed over the sandhills, looking
everywhere for his lost cow.

Deeper and deeper into the hills he wandered.

And that is when he found it.

A cave.

Nearly hidden in the hillside.

Cesario pulled aside the brush at the cave's entrance and peered in.

It was dark, but cool and inviting on this hot day.

And mysterious, as all cave's are.

Once Cesario had entered the cave he became amazed.

The walls were covered with drawings of animals.

Drawings such as the Ancient Indian peoples made.

Staring at this art he moved deeper into the cave,

but suddenly something more amazing than the paintings caught his
eye.

There, standing in the middle of the cave floor,

was a large wooden chest.

"Adios Mio!" Could it be?

Cesario pried open the lid.

He lifted it high.

"It WAS! GOLD!"

The trunk was filled to the brim with gold.

Gold coins. Gold nuggets. Gold dust.

Gold . . . Gold . . . Gold.

Cesario danced with delight.

He was laughing and yelling at the same time.

"I'm RICH! I'm RICH! RICO! RICO! RICO!"

He couldn't stop chortling with joy.

Then suddenly he heard laughter echoing throughout the cave.

"It must be the echos of my own laughter," he thought.

But he stopped laughing and stood listening for a moment.

It was then that a loud voice came thundering from the back of the cave . . .

"TODO O NADA!"

"All . . . or Nothing."

"Todo o nada?

That's easy.

I'll take TODO!

I'll take it ALL!"

Cesario stooped to lift the huge chest.

Impossible.

It was so heavy he could not even budge it.

"Then I'll take all I can carry."

He filled his pockets.

He filled his sombrero.

He pulled up his shirt tail and filled his shirt tail with gold.

"That's all for now.

That will have to do."

Cesario stumbled toward the cave opening.

But suddenly the cave floor began to shake.

The walls began to tremble.

A rumbling was heard and rocks fell closing the cave's entrance.

Cesario was left standing in the dark, clutching his gold.

"Todo o NADA

Todo o NADA"

"Yes, yes, I understand.

I'll take NADA."

Cesario dumped the gold from his sombrero.
Cesario dropped his shirt tail and let the gold fall to the floor.
Cesario reached into his pockets, pulled out handfulls of gold and
    threw it to the floor . . .
carefully leaving a *few* coins in the bottom of each pocket.

"See . . . NADA . . ."
Cesario held out his empty hands.
    "Let me out now."

But the voice was not so easily fooled.
    "Todo o NADA.
    Todo o NADA!"

    "All right, all right."

Cesario pulled out his pockets and dumped the last few coins to the
    floor.
    "NOW will you let me out?"

The floor of the cave began to shake.
The walls began to tremble.
The roaring of stones falling away was heard.
And once again the cave's mouth was open.

Cesario ran out into the daylight.
        "THAT was a narrow escape.
        I barely got out with my LIFE."

But as soon as he had calmed down a bit,
the GREED overtook him.

"If I go home and get my wheelbarrow . . .
I could take TODO!"

Cesario took off his shirt and scrambled up a nearby hill to tie it to a
bush.

"That will mark the spot so I can be sure to find the cave
again."

Cesario hurried home.

He loaded a stout rope into his wheelbarrow and started back for the
hills.

If you have ever tried to push a wheelbarrow over rugged, sandy ground
you will know that Cesario did not have an easy time of it.

Down ravines, over hills, Cesario pushed and dragged his
wheelbarrow.

He was sweating and groaning in the hot sun.

At last he reached the spot where he thought the cave had been.

He found nothing.

No shirt . . . no cave.

"It must have been down another ravine."

Pushing his barrow, he moved on.

Down another ravine.

Over another hill.

Still no cave.

All day he searched, dragging his wheelbarrow about in that hot sun.

Long after dark he made his way back to the village and stumbled
into the cantina.

"You would not BELIEVE what has happened to me today."
he told his friends.

And when they gathered around, he told them the story of the cave of
treasure and the voice which boomed "TODO O NADA".

"Cesario, you have been out in the hot sun too long,"
laughed his friends.

28

"Your mind is playing tricks on you."
No one would even believe such a story.
"But it is TRUE!" swore Cesario.
"Just this morning these very pockets were full of GOLD!"
And he pulled his pockets inside out to show them as he spoke.

A silence fell on the room.
Everyone stared at those pockets of Cesario.
They were shining in the lamplight.
Those pockets were lined with *gold dust*.

For months after that night the hills around that place were covered
    with men pushing wheelbarrows.
They climbed over every inch of those hills, searching for the
    treasure cave.
But it was never found.

It is there still.
I have a map.
If you would like to go down there and search, you can borrow it.

There's gold buried in the hills,
down around Brownsville, Texas.
So they say.

NOTES ON TELLING

Do not try to tell this story in the exact words I use here.

Just tell it as if it is something you heard about which you believe to be true
and narrate the events as well as you can remember. Make the "Todo o Nada" deep
and sonorous. Remember it would be echoing throughout the cave.

The children are usually interested in treasure maps after hearing this and
would enjoy looking at books with such maps or drawing their own. It might also
be a good time to get out a map of Texas. Brownsville is in the southernmost point

of Texas. Santa Cruz is up the Rio Grande several miles, actually, near Rio Grande, but is too small to appear on most maps. My source also mentioned sunken Spanish galleons off Padre Island. You might look for that on your map too, as it lies just east of Brownsville.

COMPARATIVE NOTES

Retold from "Todo o Nada/ All or Nothing" in *Stories That Must Not Die* by Juan Sauvageau, p. 67–70. A variant appears in *Flour From Another Sack and Other Proverbs, Folk Beliefs, Tales, Riddles amd Recipes* by Mark Glazer, p. 188. The variant was collected in Mission, Texas, and is told of a cave in Mexico where a shrine to the Virgen del Chorrito is located.

Stith Thompson motifs assigned to such treasure tales are N512 *Treasure in underground chamber (cavern)* and N553 *Tabus in effect while treasure is being unearthed*. The tale bears some similarities to Type 676 *Open Sesame*.

CHARRO DAYS IN BROWNSVILLE, TEXAS
AND MATAMOROS, MEXICO

Brownsville, Texas, and Matamoros, Mexico, lie just across the Rio Grande River from each other. Each February the two cities join in a civic celebration they call "Charro Days." Charro Days is a celebration of pride in the history of this region. The Charros, Mexican Cowboys, are stunning figures in their elaborately embroidered suits and broad brimmed hats, with their silver spurs and trimmings. A parade features horseback riders in their elaborate traditional costume, children in a variety of folk dancing costumes, and floats. Folk dance performances feature children from each school, colorfully dressed. Each class selects a folk dance to learn and prepares costumes appropriate for that dance. The towns decorate themselves with red, green, and white banners (the Mexican national colors) and festive foods are sold. Dance competitions are held. And a jalapeño pepper eating contest is featured! Also an exciting *grito* competition is held. The *grito* is a stirring shout performed by a man.

SUGGESTIONS FOR A CHARRO DAYS CELEBRATION

Decorate the classroom with red, green, and white streamers, flags, or lacy paper cuttings. To make paper cuttings use red, green, and white tissue paper squares.

Fold the squares in half, then in half again, then again. Snip triangles and other shapes from the folded papers. Open. Suspend a string across the room and tape your lacy paper cuttings to the string so they can flutter in the breeze.

Learn a simple Mexican folk dance. Music and directions for "La Raspa" appear in *Dancing Games for Children of All Ages* by Esther L. Nelson (New York: Sterling, 1972), pp. 44–45.

Snack on Mexican treats— sample jalapeño peppers!

Have a *grito* contest. Practice shouting the most stirring call. The voice should reverberate and be heard from far off. The traditional *grito* sounds something like "Aaayy-ay-ay-ay-ay-ayy!" The *grito* shouter takes a special stance as he lets out his call.

FOR MORE ACTIVITIES

"Mexican and Mexican-American Cultures" in *Cultural Awareness for Children* by Judy Allen, Earldene McNeil, and Velma Schmidt (New York: Addison-Wesley, 1992). Activities for a preschool unit on Mexican-American customs. Some could be adapted for elementary grades. Instructions for a very simple "La Raspa" dance.

BOOKS TO SHARE

Fiesta! by Beatriz McConnie Zapater. Illus. by Jose Ortega. (New York: Simon & Schuster, 1993). An Hispanic festival which celebrates many cultures is shown.

Fiesta! Cinco de Mayo by June Behrens. Photos by Scott Taylor. (Chicago: Children's Press, 1978). Historical background on the May 5, 1862 victory of the Mexican army over the French, and a look at Cinco de Mayo celebrations in the U.S.

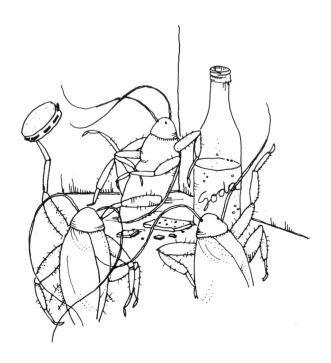

POULE AND ROACH

A Louisiana French tale.

There once was a hen, who married a cockroach.
A bad match you might say.
but the hen was in love.

The hen, because she was French, was called *Poule*.
And the cockroach, of course, was called *Roach*.

What a wedding feast they had.
Now Roach was the best drummer in those parts, so of course Roach
    played his drums for the party.
        Bim Bam Bom!
        Tabiddi Biddi Bom!

Bim Bam Bom!
Tabiddi Biddi Bom!
How they did DANCE to that drumming!
They sang and danced until dawn.
The day after the wedding Poule and Roach slept in to recover.

But the NEXT day, SIX A.M., Poule jumped out of bed.
She did her deep knee bends.
"A one and a two and a one and a two . . ."
And she was ready to GO.
"Wake up, Roach.
Time to go to the FARM!"

Roach turned over in bed.
He began to groan.
"Oh, wife, my dear," he said.
"I have SUCH a tummy ache today.
I don't believe I can go with you.
Go ahead without me."

"Oh that's too bad, hubby.
I hope you feel better soon."

Poule took her rake and her hoe and went off to the farm.
"Ta doodle doodle doo
Ta doodle doodle doo
I'm off to the farm
Ta doodle doodle doo"

But as soon as she was gone,
Roach jumped out of bed.

He grabbed his drum
and he began to play.
>Bim Bam Bom!
>Tabiddi Biddi Bom
>Bim Bam Bom!
>Tabiddi Biddi Bom!

Then Roach had a bright idea.
Roach grabbed the phone and called all of his roach buddies.
>"Hey, Roach Buddies!
>Come on over!
>Poule's gone!
>We can PARTY!"

Soon cockroaches came running down the road from the right.
Cockroches came running down the road from the left.
Cockroaches came running down the road in the middle.
Some brought sodapop.
Some brought crackers.
Some brought musical instruments.

All day long that house rocked with the sound of Roach's drum.
>Bim Bam Bom
>Tabiddi biddi bom!
>Bim Bam Bom
>Tabiddi Biddi Bom!

How they danced!
But along about four o'clock Roach stopped the party.
>"Everybody clean up quick before Poule gets home!"

Those roaches scurried around that house.
They threw the empty bottles in the garbage can.
They threw the empty cracker boxes in the garbage can.

Then they packed up their musical instruments and left the house.
Some ran up the road to the right.
Some ran up the road to the left.
Some ran up the road in the middle.
Roach jumped back into bed and pulled up the covers.

After a while Poule came home.
>"Ta doodle doodle doo . . ."

Roach was in bed groaning.
>"Oh I felt so sick. All day."

>"Poor Roach," said Poule.
>"I will make you some soup."

She stirred up her special soup.
She fed it to him with a spoon.

Next morning, SIX A.M.!
Poule jumped out of bed.
>"A one and a two and a one and a two. . . ."

>"Come on, Roach!
>Time to get to work!"

Roach just turned over and groaned.
>"Oh, wife, my dear.
>My tummy ache is worse than ever today.
>You go on to work without me."

>"Poor hubby.
>I hope you feel better later."

Poule took her little rake and her little hoe and started up the road to
the farm.

>"Ta doodle doodle doo
>Ta doodle dooddle doo
>I'm off to the farm
>Ta doodle doodle doo"

As soon as Poule was gone, Roach jumped out of bed.
He grabbed his drum and began to play.

>Bim Bam Bom!
>Tabiddi Biddi Bom!
>Bim Bam Bom!
>Tabiddi Biddi Bom!

Roach picked up the phone and called all of his friends.

>"Hey, Roach Buddies!
>Come on over!
>Poule is gone.
>We can PARTY!"

Cockroaches came running down the road from the right.
Cockroaches came running down the road from the left.
Cockroaches came running down the road in the middle.
Some brought sodapop.
Some brought crackers.
Some brought musical instruments.
All day that house rocked to their singing.

>Bim Bam Bom!
>Tabiddi Biddi Bom!
>Bim Bam Bom!
>Tabiddi Biddi Bom!

At four o'clock Roach sent them home.
       "Clean up the trash, quick.
       Get out of here before Poule comes home!"
Those cockroaches scurried around.
The put the empty bottles in the garbage can.
The put the empty cracker boxes in the garbage can.
They packed up their musical instruments and left.
Some ran up the road to the right.
Some ran up the road to the left.
Some ran up the road in the middle.
Roach jumped back in bed and pulled up the coveres.

Pretty soon Poule came home
       "Ta doodle doodle doo . . ."

Roach was groaning.
       "Oooh, I felt so sick all day."

       "Poor little husband.
       I will make you some soup."
Poule stirred up her special soup.
She fed it to Roach with a spoon.

Next morning, SIX A.M.!
Poule jumped out of bed.
       "A one and a two and a one and a two . . ."

       "Come along, husband.
       Time to go to the farm."

But Roach was still groaning.
       "Oh, my tummy still hurts, wife.

It hurts worse than ever today.
You'd better go without me."

"I'm sorry hubby dear.
Maybe you'll feel better later."

Poule took her little rake and her little hoe and started out.
    "Ta doodle doodle . . ."
But as she went out the gate she noticed the garbage can.
It looked like it was full of *bottles*.
She took off the lid.
What did she see?
Pop bottles!
Cracker boxes!
    "Where did THIS come from?
    Something is going on here."

Poule went down the road.
    "Ta doodle doddle doo . . .
    Ta doodle doodle doo. . . ."
She doubled back and hid behind the house.
    Ta doodle doodle doo. . . ."
She leaned on her hoe and waited.
To see what would happen.

Pretty soon
DOWN the road from the left came cockroaches!
DOWN the road from the right came cockroaches!
DOWN the road from the middle came cockroaches!
Some were carrying sodapop.
Some were carrying crackers.

38

Some were carrying musical instruments.
ALL of them ran right into HER house!

Then the racket started!
> BIM BAM BOM!
> TABIDDI BIDDI BOM!
> BIM BAM BOM!
> TABIDDI BIDDI BOM!

Poule waited until that party had really heated up.
Then she stepped into the doorway.
> "So THIS is what you do while *I* am working!"

Poule began to *peck* at those cockroaches.
> "PECK . . . PECK . . . PECK . . . PECK . . ."

They *scurried* to get away.
Some ran up the road to the right.
Some ran up the road to the left.
Some ran up the road in the middle.
They left their sodapop.
They left their crackers.
They even left their musical intruments.
The house was EMPTY.

Then Poule turned to Roach.
> "So THIS is how your tummy hurts!
> Let's see how it feels when *I* get through with you!"

And she began to peck at Roach.
> "PECK! PECK! PECK!"

The last I saw of them Roach was running up the road in the middle
with Poule right behind him . . . pecking all the way.

Now that is why, if a cockroach EVER crosses the door into a
    chickenhouse . . . those hens just JUMP on it and PECK it up!
It's because they remember the way Roach acted that time he was
    married to Poule.

NOTES ON TELLING

The children can drum with you on Roach's "Tabiddi biddi bom." Fingertips
drumming lightly on desks works fine for the classroom. But when the final party
takes place it's hard not to really cut loose and pound.

Poule is very perky. Do her little deep knee bends with her and sing jauntily
as she goes off to work. On the third morning she is getting a little suspicious and
doesn't say goodbye to Roach quite as heartily as before. And of course her "Ta
doodle doodle doos" trail off as she quietly goes behind to hide. In my own telling
the children often help me stir Poule's soup with her. I usually offer it to one
audience member, pretending that person is Roach and waiting until they drink it
up. It is also fun to walk around pecking on various audience members when Poule
takes off after the cockroaches. But use such devices only if they feel comfortable
to you.

Of course, the cockroaches should be bringing beer and hard liquor to the
party, not pop and crackers. You can adjust this when telling to adult audiences.

COMPARATIVE NOTES

This tale is retold from a much briefer variant in *Fools and Rascals: Louisiana
Folktales* by Calvin Andre Claudel (Baton Rouge, LA: Legacy Publishing, 1978).
The author says the story is from Orleans Parish and was originally heard in French
Guiana.

Stith Thompson Motif A2494.13.3 *Enmity between fowl and cockroach*
cites one variant, from Antigua.

This tale seems related to Stith Thompson Motif K343.3 *Companian sent
away so that rascal may steal common food supply.* Thompson cites sources from
India, Cameroon, Georgia, Virginia, South Carolina, and the Cape Verde Islands.

The tale reminds one also of K372 *Playing Godfather,* the tale best known
for it's Grimm variant "Half Gone" in which a cat and mouse store away a crock of
butter. The cat leaves repeatedly to attend a christening and returns saying the

babies were named "Part Gone," "Half Gone," and "All Gone". In fact the cat has been eating up the butter.

Compare "Poule and Roach" also to Ashley Bryan's Montserrat tale *The Cat's Purr* (New York: Atheneum, 1985).

MARDI GRAS

Mardi Gras, literally Fat Tuesday, is the last chance for Christians to feast and party before the six-week-long Lenten season begins on Ash Wednesday. The official Mardi Gras season stretches from Twelfth Night, January 6, to Shrove Tuesday. However the most riotous celebrating takes place on Shrove Tuesday itself.

In New Orleans Mardi Gras is celebrated with several parades and balls. Each of the various Mardi Gras clubs, called *krewes,* selects its own theme each year and stages its own parade featuring a king riding high on a float. From the float, costumed members of the *krewe* toss plastic necklaces and trinkets to the audience, while the onlookers shout "Give me something, Mister!" The *krewe* return to their own headquarters after the parade for their own elegant and private ball.

The Mardi Gras colors are gold, green, and purple. Costumes and masks are worn by anyone wanting to join in the fun and the streets are crowded with revelers.

Most elaborate of the costumes may be those worn by the Mardi Gras Indians, actually black *tribes* which dance through the streets showcasing elaborate feathered headresses and costumes. Over twenty tribes exist. They work for months sewing the costumes and practicing the dances. Each tribe follows its own route dancing through the streets during Mardi Gras, and whenever two Chiefs meet, a dancing competition occurs, each showing off his skills and costume in an effort to best the other.

Out in the country, the Cajun Mardi Gras is equally exciting but quite different. Revellers ride from house to house demanding chickens for a community gumbo. They are provided with live chickens and drinks, and everyone shows up later for a huge party with music and dancing long into the night.

SUGGESTIONS FOR A MARDI GRAS CELEBRATION

Decorate your space with Mardi Gras colors—purple, green, and gold streamers.

Make a Mardi Gras mask. Cut a twelve-inch length of wooden dowel. Glue this to one side of an inexpensive eye-mask. Or cut an eye-mask from heavy poster paper or half of a paper plate. Decorate the mask with purple, green, and gold sequins, glitter, ribbons, and feathers.

Make *capuchons,* cone-shaped party hats. Roll stiff metallic paper into cones and glue or tape, then punch holes on the sides and attach ribbons so the hat can be tied onto the head. Decorate with glitter and sequins.

Parade around to show off your masks and/or *capuchons.*

Play recordings of New Orleans jazz and dance in your masks. Serve a King's Cake. This is a cake baked in a ring pan and iced in purple, green, and gold. A plastic baby doll is baked into the cake. Traditionally, whoever gets the doll must hold the next party of the Mardi Gras season. This cake is served at every party from January 6 to Shrove Tuesday. Wrap your doll in foil so it does not pollute the cake, or substitute another object as the "prize".

FOR INFORMATION ON MARDI GRAS IN NEW ORLEANS

"Shrove Tuesday or Mardi Gras" in *The Folklore of American Holidays* by Hennig Cohen and Tristram Potter Coffin (Detroit: Gale Research, 1987), p. 77–91.

BOOKS TO SHARE

Carl's Masquerade by Alexandra Day (New York: Farrar, Straus, and Giroux, 1992). Carl carries Baby to a masked party.

Nini at Carnaval by Errol Lloyd (New York: Crowell, 1979). A Haitian girl lacks a costume for the Carnaval parade.

Vejigantes Masquerade by Lulu DeLacre (New York: Scholastic, 1993), A Puerto Rican boy makes his own costume for Carnaval.

FIVE THREADS

A folktale from Iraq.

INTRODUCTION

In Islamic custom the month of Ramadan is a fasting month. Devout Muslims do not eat or drink from sunrise to sunset each day during this entire month.

STORY

On the last day of Ramadan Papa Sparrow and Mama Sparrow
    planned a feast to break the month's long fast.

Papa Sparrow flew to the market and returned with SEVEN grains of wheat!

"Look, Mama, we will have such a feast tonight!"

Papa Sparrow flew off to invite the guests.

While he was gone, Mama Sparrow tidied up the nest.

She arranged the seven grains of wheat for the feast.

Then she sat down to wait.

She waited and waited but Papa Sparrow did not return.

And then . . . the moon came up.

"Now I can break my fast!

Now I can eat!"

But Papa still was not home.

Poor Mama Sparrow had not eaten all day.

She had been fasting for a whole month.

She was very hungry.

"I believe I will just eat one wheat grain.

Papa will not mind."

She ate one grain of wheat.

It was delicious, but it barely stopped her hunger.

"Perhaps just one more. . . ."

"Papa and his friends must be dallying somewhere.

Perhaps someone else is giving them food."

She ate three more grains of wheat.

Then without thinking she popped one more into her mouth and chewed it.

"Oh my. There is only one grain of wheat left.

There is no use leaving ONE grain.

I might as well eat it too."

And she did.

Just then Papa Sparrow arrived with his friends.

"Mama! Mama! Bring out the feast.
Our guests have arrived!"

"Oh, Papa. I am afraid you will be angry with me.
I was so hungry.
I ate the grains of wheat."

"You ATE the grains of wheat?
Not all SEVEN grains of wheat!"
"Well . . . yes."
Papa Sparrow was SO angry.
He lost his temper completely.
"Go HOME to your FATHER!
Go HOME to your FATHER!
Go HOME to your FATHER!"
Three times he spoke these angry words.

Poor Mama Sparrow trembled at his anger.
She packed her little bag.
She flew home to her father's nest.

Papa's friends went home, and Papa went to bed alone.

In the morning he awoke.
"Good morning, Mama."
Mama Sparrow was not there.
"I sent her home.
Now I MISS her.
Oh, dear."

Papa Sparrow flew to the nest of Mama Sparrow's father.
He perched on a branch near the nest and he called to her:

45

"Äna! Äna!
Bint as sähira.
Äna! Äna!
Bint as näqira.

Dear little feathered wife,
with your cute little beak.
Come home, come home
to your sweet little hubby."

His wife stuck her beak out of the nest and glared at him.
"Go AWAY!
I won't come home."

She pulled her head back inside her father's nest and she didn't look
out again all day.

Papa Sparrow had to go home and sleep alone that night.

The next morning he flew back to the nest of Mama Sparrow's father.
He perched on a branch and called:
"Äna! Äna!
Bint as sähira.
Äna! Äna!
Bint as näqira.

Dear little feathered wife
with your cute little beak
Come home, come home
to your sweet little hubby."

Mama Sparrow stuck her beak out of her father's nest and peered at
him.

46

"Go AWAY.

I won't come home."

She pulled her head back inside the nest and did not look out again.

Poor Papa Sparrow had to go home and sleep alone that night too.

The next morning, Papa Sparrow said to himself,
> "I made Mama Sparrow SO mad.
> I must think of something VERY lovely to make Mama
> Sparrow feel GLAD again."

He went to the market and asked the seamstress for five threads.
> "Do you have a red thread?"

She gave him a red thread.

It was bright and beautiful.
> "Do you have a blue thread?"
> "Yes! Bright as the sea!"
> "Do you have a green thread?"
> "Green as the new wheat fields."
> "Do you have a yellow thread?"
> "As bright as the morning sun."
> "Do you have a lilac thread?"
> "Oh the lovely shine of that lilac thread!"

Papa Sparrow carried the five threads to the nest of Mama Sparrow's
father.

He perched on the branch.
> "Äna! Äna!
> Bint as sähira.
> Äna! Äna!
> Bint as näqira.
>
> Sweet little feathered wife.
> with your cute little beak.

47

Come home, come home
to your dear little hubby."

And then he called:
"I BROUGHT you something."

Mama Sparrow poked her head out of the nest.
"I brought you a RED thread!
I brought you a BLUE thread!
I brought you a GREEN thread!
I brought you a YELLOW thread!
I brought you a LILAC thread!"
Mama Sparrow saw those five threads shining like jewels in the
sunlight.
What do you think she said?
"Oh PAPA! THANK you THANK you THANK you!"
She flew right down and covered him with kisses.
She snatched up those five brightly colored threads and flew back to
their nest.
There she wove the threads into the nest until it was SO beautifully
decorated.
Meanwhile Papa Sparrow flew off and brought back seven grains of
wheat AND his friends.
What a party they had that night in that nest!

Sometimes if you make someone very mad
you have to do something very nice
to make them glad again.

NOTES ON TELLING

Papa Sparrow is very stern when he sends Mama Sparrow home to her father. He
is very plaintive when he tries to woo her back. Sometimes I have him say

"Won't you come home to your hubby, hubby, hubby?" and shake his feathers appealingly.

I bring five bright lengths of embroidery floss and present them one at a time when he gives his gifts to Mama Sparrow.

COMPARATIVE NOTES

Retold from "The Sparrow and His Wife" in *Folk-tales of Iraq* by E. S. Stevens (New York: Benjamin Blom, 1931), pp. 12–13.

Papa Sparrow's entire chant as given in Steven's text is:
    Ana! Ana!
    Bint as sāhira
    Bint as nāqira
    Bint ābul rīsh wal manqara
    Jīnā nsālah marrtna
    Ta'tūna illa naradd lil wara!

Which he translates as:
    It is I, it is I!
    Little witch, little pecker!
    Little feathered and billed wife,
    I want you back!
    I want you home!

When he brings the threads he calls:
    Bil āhmari, bil ākhdhari,
    Bil āsfari bil māwi bil lilāqi
    Ta'tūna illa naradd lil wara?
    A red, and a green,
    a yellow, a blue, and a lilac I have brought.
    Will you give her to me, or shall I return without her?

In Islamic tradition, if a husband says to his wife "Woman, I divorce you!" three times, the divorce is official. This is what Papa Sparrow said in the Steven's text. I softened it, since divorce is a painful subject to many of our children.

49

ID AL-FITR/ Eed Al-Fittir

An Islamic tradition.

The holy month of Ramadan ends with a feast, the Id Al-Fitr. Ramadan will begin circa February 1 in 1995. The month of Ramadan begins approximately eleven days earlier each year on the western calendar. Thus the fasting month gradually moves through the entire year. Muslims do not eat or drink from sunrise to sunset during this entire month. Obviously this will cause increased hardships when Ramadan falls during the hottest months of the year.

Each evening during Ramadan one may break fast as soon as it so dark that one cannot tell a black thread from a white thread. And each morning the fast begins as soon as it is light enough to distinguish a white thread from a black thread. On the last day of the month of Ramadan the month long fast may be broken on the first sighting of the moon. If it happens to be cloudy, the fast might have to be extended another day. The religious leaders watch for the moon and announce the offical sighting. Thus Id Al-Fitr will fall approximately one month after the beginning of Ramadan.

The holy month of fasting, Ramadan, ends with great rejoicing in the Id Al-Fitr. This is a time of feasting and celebration as well as a time of worship. Villages may sponsor fairs with small ferris wheels, swings, merry-go-rounds and puppet shows for the children. Everyone is dressed in festive clothing.

SUGGESTIONS FOR AN ID AL-FITR CELEBRATION

Remember to plan your celebration to occur AFTER Ramadan, not during the fasting month.

Tell the story of "The Five Threads." To extend this story I give each child a round piece of paper about 4" in diameter. I have pre-cut slashes diagonally into the edges of this circle. The children fold up the sides of the circle and weave strands of embroidery floss in the five colors of our story into the slashes, creating a nest decorated with brightly colored threads.

The fast is usually broken with a light sweet such as figs or dates and some fruit juice. Prepare a special snack of figs or dates and fruit juice. After you have broken your fast, you might feast on salted nuts or baklava pastry.

If a playground with swings is nearby, decorate the swings with streamers and swing to celebrate.

FOR MORE INFORMATION ABOUT RAMADAN AND ID AL-FITR

"Ramadan" in *Folklore of World Holidays* by Margaret Read MacDonald (Detroit: Gale Research, 1992), pp. 162–172. and "Id Al-Fitr (The Little Feast) pp. 173–177.

ACTIVITIES

"Arabic Materials and Programs" by Julie Corsaro in *Venture into Cultures: A Resource Book of Multicultural Materials & Programs* by Carla D. Hayden, editor. (Chicago: American Library Association, 1992), pp. 19–36.

"Iraq" in *Children's Games from Many Lands* by Nina Millen (New York: Friendship Press, 1964). A singing game to play.

BOOKS TO SHARE

Count Your Way Through the Arab World by Jim Haskins. Illus. by Dana Gustafson (Minneapolis: Carolrhoda, 1987). Numbers 1–10 in Arabic with brief information on the Arab world.

Tell the story "Three Questions" from *Once the Hodja* by Alice Geer Kelsey. Illus. by Frank Dobias (New York: McKay, 1943), pp. 100–107. The Hodja preaches in the mosque for three weeks in this humorous tale from Turkey.

Tell the story "Little Cricket's Marriage" from *Look Back and See: Lively Tales for Gentle Tellers* by Margaret Read MacDonald (New York: H.W. Wilson, 1991), pp. 55–60. This Palestinian Arab tale is also popular in Iraq.

THE PUMPKIN CHILD

A folktale from Iran.

There once was an old woman who longed to have a child.
She prayed to Allah.

"Please grant me a child.
I would love a child so,
even if it were nothing more than a little pumpkin."

One morning when she awoke she heard something bumping at her
door.
The old woman opened the door . . .
and there was a little green pumpkin.

The pumpkin rolled right into her house and began to roll around and
around the old woman.

"Pumpity pumpity pumpity pumpity"

Then the pumpkin stopped in front of the old woman and rocked back
and forth.

"Pum . . . pum . . . pum . . . pum . . ."

"I believe this little pumpkin wants me to pick it up."

The old woman bent over and picked up the little pumpkin.

As soon as it was in her arms, the pumpkin began to whimper like a
tiny baby.

"Don't cry little one.

Don't cry little pumpkin."

The old woman began to rock the pumpkin and comfort it.

Soon the pumpkin stopped crying and began to breathe softly.

"Annn. . . annn. . . annnn. . . ."

The little pumpkin was asleep.

"Why it is just like a *baby*!" said the old woman.

"This pumpkin can be my CHILD!"

She made a little cradle in the corner and laid the pumpkin in it.

She rocked the pumpkin.

She sang to the pumpkin.

From then on she cared for that pumpkin as if it were her true child.

She would take the pumpkin out of it's cradle every day and polish it
with a clean white cloth.

The pumpkin was even *better* than a baby . . . she didn't have to
change its diapers!

The pumpkin began to grow.

53

Soon it was big enough to get out of it's cradle and roll around the
house during the day.

"Pumpity . . . pumpity . . . pumpity . . ."

The little pumpkin would bump into the furniture and get into the old
woman's way.

But she enjoyed it's company.

When it was even bigger, the old woman took the pumpkin out into
the garden to play.

The pumpkin loved to hide from the old woman.

It would run down a row of vegetables and hide behind the corn.

"I will find you, Little Pumpkin!

Here I come, " the old woman would call.

And she would peer here and there until she spotted the little
pumpkin.

"THERE you are!"

The little pumpkin giggled.

It liked that game.

But the little pumpkin began to misbehave.

She would hide her mother's things around the house.

One day her mother could not find her silk scarf anywhere.

"Little Pumpkin, have you seen my scarf?

Wherever could it be?"

The little pumpkin was *sitting* on her mother's scarf the whole time.

"Little Pumpkin, move over just a bit . . .

THERE is my scarf!

You naughty little pumpkin!"

The mother decided to send the pumpkin to school so she would learn
how to behave.

So the mother polished the little pumpkin one morning and sent her
    off down the road to the school.
By this time the pumpkin had grown quite a bit.
She was even starting to turn from green to orange!

Off down the road she went.
        "Pumpity . . . pumpity . . . pumpity . . ."
She rolled right into the school and sat down at a desk.

And sure enough . . .
the school teacher was *very* strict.
        "Children! Sit up straight!
        You TOO, Little Pumpkin."

        "Children! Behave yourselves!
        You TOO, Little Pumpkin."

Soon she had learned how to behave very well.

Every evening Little Pumpkin would roll back to her home.
        "Pumpity . . . pumpity . . . pumpity . . ."

The pumpkin grew larger and larger.
And her skin turned a beautiful orange color.
She was almost completely grown!

Now on her way to school, Pumpkin had to pass the king's palace.
The young prince often would lean out of a window and watch the
    others going to school.
He wished that he could go to school with them for he was lonely.

But he had to stay in the palace and have his lessons with a private
tutor.

One day the prince noticed the little pumpkin rolling to school.

"Now there is something strange," he thought.

"Where can a *pumpkin* be going?"

That evening he saw her rolling back home again.

After that he watched each day for the pumpkin.

Finally he decided to follow the pumpkin and see where it went.

He climbed down from his window and hurried along behind her.

"Pumpity . . . pumpity . . . pumpity . . ." the pumpkin
rolled down the road.

When she came to a grape arbor the little pumpkin looked around to
see if anyone was watching . . . then she rolled right into the
grape arbor and rested in the shade.

The prince hid himself and watched to see what she would do.

In a moment the pumpkin began to shake . . . and suddenly it split in
half!

Out of the pumpkin stepped a beautiful girl!

She was as beautiful as the full moon.

The prince fell in love immediately.

The girl stood on tiptoe and picked a bunch of grapes.

Then she sat down in the shade and ate them slowly.

When she had finished, she stepped back into her pumpkin shell.

The pumpkin closed again.

And the pumpkin rolled off down the road.

"Pumpity . . . pumpity . . . pumpity."

The prince ran home.

He went straight to the royal jeweler.

"Make me a gold ring," he commanded.

"I must have it by tomorrow."

So the jeweler made him a ring of gold.

The next day the prince took the ring and hurried to the spot where
   he had seen the beautiful girl.
He hid himself behind the grape vines and waited.
As soon as school was over, the pumpkin came rolling down the
   road.
   "Pumpity . . . pumpity . . . pumpity . . ."
When she came alongside the grape arbor the pumpkin looked
   around.
Then she rolled into the arbor and rested in the shade.
In a moment the pumpkin began to shake, the pumpkin split open
and the beautiful girl stepped out.

Standing on tiptoe, the girl picked a bunch of grapes.
Then she sat down in the shade to eat them.
The prince watched her for a moment.
Then he got ready . . .
He LEAPED from his hiding place,
looked straight into her eyes,
placed the gold ring on her middle finger,
pulled it off again,
and ran out of the grape arbor and back up the road.

When he reached the palace he went straight to his mother.
   "Mother! Mother! I have found the girl I want to marry!
   This gold ring will fit her finger.
   You must find her for me!"

His mother called her servants and sent them out to search the
   countryside.
   "Somewhere in this village lives a girl whose middle finger
      will fit this ring.
   She is to be the Prince's bride."

The servants went to each house.

"Do you have a young girl here?
Let me see her middle finger . . .
Sorry. You are not the one."

"Is there a young girl at this house?
Hold out your middle finger please.
Never mind. It's not you."

Eventually they came to the home of the old woman.

"Do you have a young girl in your household?"

"Well, yes I do.
But she is a . . . pumpkin."

"A *pumpkin*?
Is this a joke?"

"No. She is a pumpkin.
See how lovely she is."

The pumpkin rolled out.
But the servants had already turned to go.

"Never mind.
We are looking for a young girl whose middle finger will fit
this ring.
We aren't interested in *pumpkins*."

The pumpkin began to quiver.
Suddenly a beautiful maiden's hand popped out of the pumpkin's
side.

"What is THIS?

Should we try the ring on THIS hand?
We might as well."
And of course the ring fit perfectly.

The servants hurried home to the Queen.
"Pardon us, your majesty.
We have found a hand to fit this ring.
But it is the hand of a . . . *pumpkin.*"

"A PUMPKIN?"
The Queen called her son.
"Son I have bad news.
The ring fits only one hand in this village.
But that hand is the hand of a . . . pumpkin."

"Then I will MARRY a PUMPKIN."

So a carriage was sent for the pumpkin.
She rode off to the palace in style.
There she was fitted with a wedding dress and taken to marry the
    prince.
It was a royal wedding, but the pumpkin did look strange.
A round orange pumpkin . . . wearing a wedding dress!

The courtiers snickered when the prince put the gold ring on the hand
    of a *pumpkin.*
But the prince drew his sword and glared at them.
"HUSH! Do not laugh at my bride!
She is more lovely than ANY of you."
He swung his sword and brought it down gently on the top of the
    pumpkin . . . calling "NOW! Come out!"
The pumpkin split open!

59

Out stepped a beautiful girl . . . wearing the golden ring.

Everyone gasped at her beauty.
And the old woman, her mother, fainted away at the sight.
When she revived, she embraced her beautiful daughter.

The prince brought the old woman to live with them in the palace
 . . . and of course they all lived happily every after.

NOTES ON TELLING

Notes for telling "The Pumpkin Child" can be found on page 66.

THE OLD WOMAN IN A PUMPKIN SHELL

A folktale from Iran.

One day Pumpkin Girl and the Prince decided to visit their country
    home for a time.
While they were away in the country, Pumpkin Girl's mother decided
    to pay them a visit.
She packed a little basket with sweets for her daughter and set out.
The way was long and she had to climb a steep mountain road.
However the old woman was trudging happily along . . .
when suddenly out jumped a huge LION!
Right into her path!

"WHO ARE YOU?" roared the Lion.

61

"And where do you think you are going on MY path!"

"I'm only a poor old woman.
Going up the hill to visit my daughter."

"Bad luck for YOU, old woman.
I am going to eat you up!"

"Oh don't eat me NOW.
Look at how skinny I am.
Wait a bit until I come BACK from my daughter's house.
She is sure to feed me lots of good things there and make
     me VERY fat."

"Good idea!
I'll eat you THEN."
So the old woman went on up the hill.
She hadn't gone far however when . . .
Out leaped a huge WOLF!
Right into her path!

"WHO ARE YOU?" snarled the Wolf.
And what are you doing on MY path?"

"I'm only a poor old woman.
Going up the hill to visit my daughter."

"Bad luck for YOU, old woman.
I am going to EAT YOU UP!"

"Oh don't do that.
Look how skinny I am.

Wait until I come back from my daughter's house.
She is sure to feed me lots of good things and make me
very fat."

"Good idea.
I'll eat you on the way BACK!"

The woman continued to climb the mountain.
Suddenly . . .
Out jumped an OGRE!
Right into her Path!

"Who are YOU?" growled the Ogre.
"And what are you doing on MY path!"

"I'm only a poor old woman.
Going up the hill to visit my daughter."

"Bad luck for YOU, old woman.
I am going to eat you up!"

"Don't do that.
Look how skinny I am.
Wait until I come back from my daughter's house.
She's sure to feed me such good things and fatten me up.
You can eat me THEN."

"Good idea.
I'll eat you when you get FAT!"

So the old woman went on up the hill.

When she arrived at her daughter's house, that daughter began to feed
her and feed her . . .
just like she had said!
She stayed twenty days.
And she DID get FAT!

But when it was time to go back home she was worried.
"My dear, " she said to her daughter. "I fear for my life."
And she told about the lion and the wolf and the ogre.
"Do not worry, mother. Remember the pumpkin shell I used
to roll about in? Just step inside. You can ROLL
yourself home!"

So the old woman climbed into the pumpkin shell.

The daughter closed it tightly and gave it a little push.
Down the hill the pumpkin rolled.
"Pumpity . . . pumpity . . . pumpity . . ."
Soon it bumped into the Ogre.
"Pumpity . . . pumpity . . . BUMP!"

"WATCH where you are going, you PUMPKIN!" shouted
the Ogre.
And then he asked "Have you seen an old woman on the
path?"

"I haven't seen an old woman," answered the old woman
from inside the pumpkin, disguising her voice.
"Not here, not there, not anywhere.
But I need to get home.
"Are you strong enough to give me a little push?"
"Of COURSE I'm strong enough."

The Ogre gave the pumpkin a nudge and it started to roll down the
hill again.
"Pumpity . . . pumpity . . . pumpity . . . BUMP!"
It ran right up against the WOLF.
"WATCH where you are going you PUMPKIN!
Say, have you seen an old woman around here?"

"I haven't seen an old woman.
Not here, not there, not anywhere.
But I need to get home.
Are you strong enough to give me a little push?"

"Of COURSE I'm strong enough!"
The wolf gave the pumpkin a nudge.
Off down the hill it bounced.
"Pumpity . . . pumpity . . . pumpity . . . BUMP!"
Right up against the LION.
"Watch where you are GOING . . . you PUMPKIN!
Say, did you see an old woman on the path?"

"I haven't seen an old woman.
Not here, not there, not anywhere.
But I need to get home.
Are you strong enough to give me a little push?"

Now the Lion was King of the Beasts.
He did not like being ordered around by a mere PUMPKIN.
"You want a PUSH?
"I'll give you a PUSH."

He picked the pumpkin up, lifted it over his head, and SMASHED it
onto the ground.

The old woman came flying out of those pumpkin rinds.
She was MAD!

> "Smash MY pumpkin . . .
> You miserable, rotten beast . . .
> You mangy, stinking Lion. . . ."

The Lion thought she must be a DEMON!
He bawled in terror and ran off down the mountain.

> "Help! Help! The PUMPKIN DEMON is after me!"

"Well," said the old woman, "What a nuisance bullies are."

The old woman dusted herself off.
The she gathered up her pumpkin pieces, strolled on back home, and
    made herself such a BIG POT of pumpkin stew.
And the next time her daughter came to visit they laughed and
    laughed at those big bullies who had been fooled by a pumpkin
    shell!

NOTES ON TELLING FOR "THE PUMPKIN CHILD"

The first half of the story is bouncy and playful, as the mother raises the little pumpkin, plays with her, and sends her to school. The tone changes in the second half of the story. It becomes a classic fairy tale as the prince spies the girl and arranges the marriage.

The children may like to make a rolling motion with their hands as the pumpkin rolls "pumpity . . . pumpity . . ." Or they can rock from side to side as she rolls.

NOTES ON TELLING FOR
"THE OLD WOMAN IN A PUMPKIN SHELL"

The lion, wolf, and ogre are, of course, suitably intimidating. Remember to disguise the old woman's voice when she calls from inside the pumpkin.

Though the texts I have seen make no mention of a festival, you *could* send the old woman to visit her daughter for No Rouz if you wanted a closer festival tie-in.

These two stories can be told separately or in combination. Children enjoy having stories serialized, so you might tell one on one day and the second on another day. To tell "The Old Woman in the Pumpkin Shell" alone, simple say that an old woman went to see her daughter one day. Don't refer to the Pumpkin Girl at all. Have the daughter simply suggest rolling home in a pumpkin shell at the story's end. This tale usually appears alone, without the "pumpkin princess" tale attached.

COMPARATIVE NOTES

These stories are found in *Persian Fairy Tales* by Jaroslav Tichý, retold by Jane Carruth, pp. 24–28, and in *Persian Folk and Fairy Tales* by Anne Sinclair Mehdevi pp. 112–117.

Stith Thompson Motif T555.1 *Woman gives birth to a fruit. Can transform itself to girl* lists variants from India (gourd) and China (pumpkin). T555 *Woman gives birth to a plant* lists Italian and Persian variants. MacDonald's *Storyteller's Sourcebook* lists our Persian variant, a Philippine variant in which a baby emerges from a squash and turns his bath water to gold, and a Chaga tale from Tanganyika in which gourds turn to children and help the poor old woman. In the Japanese tale of Momotaro (T543.2.1), a helpful child is born from a peach, and in some variants of "The Snot Nose Boy" (p. 104 in this book), the child emerges from a fruit.

The "ring test" motif, H36.3 *Search for finger which fits ring,* of course reminds us of Cinderella, with it's slipper test.

The second story is similar to a tale from India which appears in many children's collections as "Lambikin". MacDonald's *Storyteller's Sourcebook* classes the tale as Motif K553.0.3 *"I'll be fatter when I return." Lambikin en route to grandmother's house thus passes jackal, vulture, tiger. Returns rolling inside a drum.* Five sources for "Lambikin" are listed. For a nicely illustrated version see *Great Children's Stories* by Frederick Richardson. MacDonald also cites a tale from Panama in which hare rolls by in a barrel (in *The Enchanted Orchard and Other Folktales of Central America* by Dorothy Sharp Carter, p. 87–90), a Nepali tale in which an old woman rolls in a gourd (*Folk Tales from Asia for Children Everywhere,* Book #2, p. 28–33), and a delightful picture book version of a Bengali tale in which an old woman rolls in a pumpkin (*The Magic Pumpkin* by Gloria Skurzynski).

You will recall that a similar motif also appears in some versions of "The

Three Little Pigs" (K891.1.1), those carrying the tagged-on ending in which the little pig goes to pick apples early in the morning and returns rolling home in a churn past the wolf.

An American tall tale also places an old woman inside a pumpkin, but this time for pure comedy. She crawls into a giant pumpkin for pie filling and it breaks loose and rolls off with her. X1411.2 *Lies about large pumpkin.* (*Tall Tales from the High Hills* by Ellis Credle, p. 16–20 and *Clever Cooks* by Ellin Greene, p. 137–142).

NO ROUZ

An Iranian tradition.

No Rouz is a thirteen-day celebration beginning March 21, on the day the sun enters Aries. This pre-Islamic holiday is an important family celebration in Iran, Iraq, Afghanistan, Kashmir, and among the Parsi families of India. The holiday is a cultural heritage from a time before Islam and does not have Islamic religious associations.

In Iran, the holiday is celebrated with a feast. Seven foods beginning with the "s" sound in Farsi are arrayed on a banquet cloth. The traditional foods used can vary as long as all begin with the "s" sound. They could include vinegar, garlic, sumac, apple, *senjed* (small date-like fuit), smoked fish, olives. A sweet pudding made of wheat (*samanu*) may also be served. Seven special objects are also arranged on the cloth. They can include a bowl of goldfish, a mirror, a jar of rosewater, a candle, a Koran, a silver item—usually a coin (*sekeh*), a hyacinth (*sanbol*). A bowl of hard-boiled eggs, yogurt, and cheese are also used, along with a *sabzeh*. The *sabzeh* is a plate of wheat or barley seeds which have been germinated in water. They are started so that the shoots are about three inches long by No Rouz, and they are tied up with a bright ribbon to highlight this green foretaste of spring. New Year cookies (*shirini*) are served and the home is made festive with spring flowers such as daffodils, tulip and cyclamens. The No Rouz items are left on display for the thirteen days of the holiday.

On the thirteenth day of the New Year, the items are removed and the *sabzeh* is taken into the countryside and thrown into fields or running water. All of the families' bad feelings are tossed out with it. Often a picnic is made of this outing and the family spends the day in the countryside.

No Rouz is also a time for visits to friends and family, and a time for the giving of gifts. In some families, Amu Nuruz (Uncle Nuruz), a Santa Claus-like character who is a symbol of spring, arrives with presents for the children. The house visits continue throughout the thirteen days of No Rouz. Elders are visited first as a sign of respect. Children often receive gifts of money during these visits . . . crisp new bills fresh from the bank. Everyone is greeted with the wish for a Happy New Year (*Aidé Shomá Mobarák*).

On the last Tuesday evening before No Rouz bonfires are lit and it is traditional to jump over the small bonfires saying "My yellowness to you, Your redness to me." This means that the leaper's sickness (yellowness) should go to the fire and the fire's redness (health) should come to the leaper.

On No Rouz children may place hardboiled eggs before them on a mirror and watch to see what happens. At the exact moment of the vernal equinox the egg should tremble as the new year begins. The exact time of the equinox is announced by the astronomers. The children are awakened for the event even if it is in the wee hours of the night, though it also sometimes falls during the day. Families also watch a citrus fruit floating in a bowl of water. It will turn in the water at the exact moment the new year begins.

SUGGESTIONS FOR A NO ROUZ CELEBRATION

Spread an attractive cloth on a table and arrange seven No Rouz items on it . . . a goldfish in a bowl, a mirror, a silver coin, a jar of rosewater, a lamp, a Koran, a bowl of hard-boiled eggs, yogurt, cheese, or a hyacinth.

Arrange seven foods beginning with the Farsi "s" sound on the cloth.

Plant a *sabzeh*. We made a very simple *sabzeh* by filling plastic margarine tubs with potting soil and planting them with wheat or grass seed. Remove the plastic tub before throwing the *sabzeh* into a stream on Day 13. For instructions on making a more traditional *sabzeh* see *Venture Into Cultures,* p. 149.

Construct a fake bonfire from red and orange crepe paper. Jump over it, calling:

"My yellowness to you.
Your redness to me!"
Or , try saying the chant in Farsi as you jump:
"Zárd yeh mán as Tó
Sorky yeh Tó as mán

Snack on apple slices and hard boiled eggs.

FOR MORE INFORMATION ON NO ROUZ

"Iran" in *Children Are Children Are Children* by Ann Cole, Carolyn Haas, Elizabeth Heller, and Betty Weinberger (Boston: Little, Brown, 1978), pp. 71–108.

"Navrouz" in *The Folklore of World Holidays* by Margaret Read MacDonald, (Detroit: Gale Research, 1992) pp. 186–187.

"Noruz" in *Festivals for You to Celebrate* by Susan Purdy (Philadelphia: J.B. Lippincott, 1969), pp. 41–42. Directions for making a *sabzeh*.

"Noruz in Iran" in *Happy New Year Round the World* by Lois S. Johnson (Chicago: Rand McNally, 1960), pp. 98–106.

"Persian Materials and Programs" by Shahla Sohail Ghadrboland in *Venture into Cultures: A Resource Book of Multicultural Materials & Programs,* edited by Carla D. Hayden (Chicago: American Library Association, 1992), pp. 142–154.

TO SHARE WITH CHILDREN

"Iran" in *Children's Games from Many Lands* by Nina Millen (New York: Friendship Press, 1964), pp. 60–63. Children's games.

"Iran" in *Happy New Year* by Emily Kelly, illus. Priscilla Kiedrowski (Minneapolis: Carolrhoda, 1984), pp. 11–17.

Uncle Nuruz by Faridh Farjam. Trans. by Ahmad Jabbari. (Costa Mesa, Calif.: Mazda, 1983). In this Iranian picture book Old Woman Winter falls asleep when Uncle Nuruz arrives on the first day of spring.

Share stories from *Once the Mullah: Persian Folk Tales* by Alice Geer Kelsey. Illus. by Kurt Werth. (New York: McKay, 1954).

ESCARGOT ON HIS WAY TO DIJON

An elaboration on a folktale from the Burgundy region of France.

INTRODUCTION

Children in France receive their Easter eggs and candies from an unusual source. It is well known that the church bells all fly off to Rome on Maundy Thursday. They do not return until three days later, on Easter Sunday. They bring with them candies and colored eggs for the children! This is obviously true, for you will not hear them pealing at all during these somber days of Lent . But on Easter Sunday morning . . . what a DIN they make! They are so happy to be back from their long flight to Rome.

Here is the story of a little snail named Escargot and his trip to Dijon for Easter Sunday mass.

STORY

One day Escargot heard the church bells ringing.

They were loud at first . . . and then fainter and fainter . . .

"This must be Maundy Thursday!" said Escargot.

"The church bells are flying off to Rome!

They won't come back until Easter Sunday.

How I would love to be in Dijon when the bells return.

I could hear the choir in the great cathedral sing the Easter morning mass!

It is a long way to Dijon city.

But if I leave right now . . . I believe I could be there by Easter.

I will DO it!"

And little Escargot started right out on the long road to Dijon.

Snails are very small . . . and they move so slowly . . .

First Escargot *pushed* his head forward . . .

then he'd *slide* . . . his body up.

Then he *pushed* his head forward . . .

and he'd *slide* . . . his body up.

Push . . . slide . . .

Push . . . slide . . .

Push . . . slide . . .

On his way

to Dijon.

Escargot moved steadily forward all morning.

"Half a day gone already!" said Escargot.

"I'd better hurry.

Dijon is a long way off.

But I'll get there.

I may be slow.
But I am *steady*."
And off he moved.

Push . . . slide . . .
Push . . . slide . . .
Push . . . slide . . .
On his way
to Dijon.

"A whole day gone!
And I've hardly moved.
Still a long way from Dijon.
But I'll get there.
I may be slow
but I am *steady*."

Push . . . slide . . .
Push . . . slide . . .
Push . . . slide . . .
On his way
to Dijon.

"Friday already!
Only two more days till Easter.
I may be slow . . .
but I am *steady*."

Push . . . slide . . .
Push . . . slide . . .
Push . . . slide . . .
On his way
to Dijon.

"Friday gone already!
I must hurry.
But I'll get there.
I may be slow
but I am *steady*."

Push . . . slide . . .
Push . . . slide . . .
Push . . . slide . . .
On his way
to Dijon.

All night he traveled.
And now Escargot could see Dijon in the distance.
The grey stone walls of the city glistened in the morning sun.
The colored tiles on the palace of the Grand Duke sparkled.
Everywhere the spires of the churches rose above the city walls,
    pointing at the sky . . .
waiting for their bells to return.
And in the very heart of the city . . .
rose the grandest spire of all . . .
the steeple of the Grand Cathedral.

"That's where I am GOING!"
Escargot was so excited.
"Tomorrow is Easter Sunday.
But I'll be there.
I may be slow . . .
but I am *steady*."

Push . . . slide . . .
Push . . . slide . . .

Push . . . slide . . .
On his way
to Dijon.

Only one day left.
He could see Dijon, but could he reach it . . .
little Escargot pushed harder than ever.
By Saturday afternoon he was so close . . . so close he could see the
  wooden gates of the city standing open far down the road before
  him.
Now in those days each city had huge wooden gates and strong stone
  walls. Every night the gatekeeper closed the wooden gates at
  sundown. Every morning at sunrise he opened them again. No
  robbers or enemies could enter the city during the night.

As Escargot started up the long road to the gates of Dijon who should
  he meet but the WOLF.
    "Bonjour, little Escargot," said the Wolf.
    "Where are you going so slowly?"
    "I am going to Dijon.
    I will be the first one at the Grand Cathedral on Easter
        Sunday morning.
    I am going to sit in the front row and hear the bells when
        they fly back from Rome.
    And I will hear the choir sing the Easter mass.
    That is where I am going."

    "What an excellent idea!" said the Wolf.
    "That is what *I* will do!
    But I am so much faster than you.
    It is *I* who will sit in the front row,
    not a creeping little snail."

75

And off trotted the Wolf.

"Oh dear." said Escargot.
"I did want to be first.
But never mind.
I won't quit yet.
I may be slow . . .
but I am *steady*."

And on he went.
Push . . . slide . . .
Push . . . slide . . .
Push . . . slide . . .
Up the hill to Dijon.

The Wolf trotted steadily up the steep hill for a while.
Then he stopped to rest.
"Plenty of time to reach Dijon," said the Wolf.
"Especially for someone as fast as ME."
And the Wolf curled up for a nap under a tree.

In a little while someone slowly pushed past the sleeping Wolf.
Push . . . slide . . .
Push . . . slide . . .
Push . . . slide . . .

"I may be slow . . .
but I am *steady* . . ."

The sun was just setting when the Wolf woke up.
"Dijon!
The gates will close!"

76

Up jumped the wolf and ran as hard as he could for the city gates.
Too late.
The gatekeeper slammed them shut . . . right in the poor wolf's
    nose.
        "BLAM!"
        Well, I will still be the first one to reach the cathedral
            tomorrow morning.
        I will sleep right here by the gate.
        As soon as it is opened I will dash in . . . run up the street
            of Dijon. . . .past the Grand Duke's palace . . . and into
            the Cathedral.
        I will be in the front row when the bells fly back from
            Rome.
        not that silly creeping snail."
So the wolf curled up by the gates and went to sleep.

And Escargot?
He was still slowly pushing his way up the hill to Dijon.
Push . . . slide . . .
Push . . . slide . . .
Push . . . slide . . .

He reached the gates of Dijon at last.
        "The gates are CLOSED!
        Oh well.
        If I can't go through.
        I will have to go over."

And Escargot began slowly to *push* himself up the great stone wall of
    the city.

Push . . . slide . . .
Push . . . slide . . .
Push . . . slide . . .

Push . . . slide . . .
Push . . . slide . . .
Push . . .
   slide . . .

He reached the top!
Now he could see all of Dijon below him!
There was the Grand Duke's palace with it's colorful tiled roof.
There was the cobbled street of the town.
There were all of the churches . . .
and there . . .
there was the Grand Cathedral itself!
     "Aaaahhhh. . . ."
Down went Escargot . . .
down the stone wall . . .
sliding SO smoothly . . .

Slip. . . .slide. . . .slip . . . slide . . . slip . . . slide . . . slide.
Up the streets of Dijon.
Slip . . . slide . . . slip . . . slide . . . slip . . . slide . . . slide.
Past the Grand Duke's palace.
     "Hello, Duke!"
Slip . . . slide . . . slip . . . slide . . . slip . . . slide . . . slide.
To the Great Cathedral.
     "Slip . . . slide . . . slip . . . slide . . ."
Down the long cathedral aisle.
     "Slip . . . slide . . . slip . . . slide . . ."
To the very front row.

And there Escargot sat.

On Easter morning he heard . . .
BELLS BELLS BELLS RINGING OVER HIS HEAD!
As all the bells of Dijon flew back from Rome,
ringing and ringing with happiness!

Out at the gates, Wolf was just waking up . . .
     "What?
     Too late?"

So the fast running Wolf arrived too late for Easter mass.
But Escargot was sitting in the very front row when the choir began
    to sing.

It is not always the fastest one who wins the race.
Sometimes slow can win . . . if slow is . . . *steady.*

NOTES ON TELLING

My introductory suggestion is optional, but you need to explain about the church
bells bringing candies and eggs to the children in France before you start the story.
You can explain about medieval cities locking their gates at sunset either before
you start the tale, or during the story. You might also discuss the Lenten season,
Maundy Thursday, Good Friday and Easter Saturday.

When Escargot moves forward I say "Push . . ." then suck in my breath
with a slurping sound . . . and add "Slide." "Push . . . slurp . . . slide . . ." The
audience does this with me, of course.

When Escargot starts up the steep wall we all strain and slow down in our
difficult pushing and sliding. As we slide down the other side we go quickly and
lightly. The pace keeps quick and easy right up through the streets of Dijon. Then
Escargot goes slowly and reverently down the aisle of the Great Cathedral.

COMPARATIVE NOTES

This story has been fabricated by enlarging on the French folktale of the escargot who raced the wolf to Dijon. The tale was related to my daughter, Jennifer, while visiting the *cave* of a winery near Dijon. The large wooden doors of the *cave* bore an intriguing carving of a snail and a wolf. When asked about this insignia, the winery owner related the story of the escargot and the wolf. He did not explain why they were going to Dijon, only that it was a race.

I have set the story at Easter and incorporated the legend of the church bells into the tale. I was fortunate to visit Dijon on Easter Sunday myself and hear the lovely Hodie of Kodaly sung at Easter morning Mass at the Cathedral of Saint Bénigne. I think Escargot would have loved it.

This is, of course, a twist on the oft repeated Aesop fable of the tortoise and the hare. MacDonald's *Storyteller's Sourcebook* cites also the La Fontaine version and a Nigerian variant of Motif K11.3 *Hare and tortoise race*. The similar tale, K11.1 *Race won by deception: relative helpers*, features a snail as main character in variants from Liberia (Mano) and Indonesia.

EASTER IN FRANCE

The Easter Sunday Mass is important in the Catholic tradition of France. The church bells are quiet from Maundy Thursday to Easter Saturday and children are told that the bells have flown to Rome to see the pope. On Easter Sunday the bells can be heard pealing the joy of the resurrection of Christ. Families tell their children that the candies and colored eggs they receive have been brought back from Rome by the church bells. Chocolate chickens and chocolate eggs are special treats at this season. And the shop windows are bright with spring floral arrangements and Easter pastries. In some parts of France, children play at tossing their eggs into the air. The one who drops and breaks an egg is the loser.

SUGGESTIONS FOR A FRENCH EASTER CELEBRATION

Look at pictures of medieval towns and medieval cathedrals. Talk about walled medieval cities, cathedral architecture.

Listen to a recording of a Mass generally performed at Easter and talk about liturgical music.

Make a paper Lenten nun. Children in France sometimes make a paper nun with seven feet. One foot is folded up each week during the Lenten season to mark the approach of Easter Sunday.

Note: Don't give the nun a mouth as a reminder that Lent is a time of fasting.

Color hard-boiled eggs, then play at tossing them into the air. The person who drops an egg and cracks it loses. Eat your losses.

Snack on chocolate eggs or bunnies.

Sing a French children's song. "Frère Jacques" tells of ringing churchbells.

TO LEARN MORE ABOUT EASTER-BELL CUSTOMS

"Easter Bells" in *Lilies, Rabbits, and Painted Eggs: the Story of Easter Symbols* by Edna Barth. (New York: Clarion, 1970), pp. 47–49. Brief information on Easter bell customs in European countries.

BOOKS ON THE MEDIEVAL CATHEDRAL

Cathedral: The Story of It's Construction by David Macaulay (Boston: Houghton Mifflin, 1973). Details of the architecture of a French Cathedral.

The Cathedral Builders by Marie-Pierre Perdrizet. Illus. by Eddy Krahenbuhl. Trans. by Mary Beth Raycroft. (Brookfield, Conn.: Millbrook Press, 1992).

Building the Medieval Cathedral by Percy Watson. (Minneapolis: Lerner, 1979).

BOOKS TO SHARE

Cathedral Mouse by Kay Chorao (N.Y.: E. P. Dutton, 1988). Lovely cathedral illustrations. A mouse and his stone-carver friend.

Madeline by Ludwig Bemelman (New York: Viking, 1939) A Catholic girls' school in Paris. Picture book.

Savez-Vous Plantez les Choux? and Other French Songs *Songs*, selected and illustrated by Anne Rockwell (Cleveland: World, 1968). Several singing games. Words and music for "Frère Jacques."

Springtime for Jeanne Marie by Françoise (New York: Scribner's, 1955). A French country girl's adventures. Picture book for the very young.

A FILM

The Red Balloon. Albert Lamorisse, film maker. MacMillan Films, 1956. 34 min. A young boy follows a red balloon through the streets of Paris.

FORGET-ME-NOT

An elaboration on a European legend.

In the begining the flowers had no names.
They asked Adam to give them each a name.
So Adam called all of the flowers together.
There were tall flowers with bright yellow faces.
There were small flowers hung with lavender bells.
There were flowers with prickly stems and huge red blooms.
All of the flowers came to be named.

But there was one tiny white flower
    so small and so pale.
No one noticed it at all.

First came a tall flower with bright red petals pointing stiffly toward
the sky.

"Marvelous!" exclaimed Adam.
"You are as red as two lips.
I will name you "tu-lips.""

Tulip strode back through the assembled flowers turning this way and
that to show off his handsome petals.

The small white flower jumped up.
"What's MY name, Adam?"
But Adam didn't see the tiny flower.

A graceful flower swept forward.
Her head was a soft bundle of curved pink petals.

"Aaah! Such loveliness!
You are beautiful!" said Adam.

The flower blushed and lowered her head.
Her face turned a deep pink.

"How becoming your blush is!" said Adam.
"I will call you ROSE and you must blush always!"

Rose swayed back through the gathered flowers, turning her lovely
head round and round for all to admire.

The little white flower jumped up again.
"What's MY name Adam?
Don't forget ME!"

But already a slender flower with a bright yellow crown had pushed
forward.

"Perfect!" exclaimed Adam.
"I will give you TWO names.
Some will call you "Daffodil"
and some will call you "Jonquil."

"He gave me TWO names!
I'm "Daffodil" AND "Jonquil.""
The flower sashayed happily off to tell her friends.

"Don't foget ME!
Don't forget ME!"
The little white flower jumped up and down at Adam's feet.
But it's voice was so soft that no one heard.

One by one the flowers came.
There was Hyacinth with her head of perfumed lavender bells,
Huge blossomed Peony,
Lilac, sweetest of them all,
and Sunflower . . . so tall that even Adam had to look up to this
    flower.

Then all were named.
The flowers strolled about saying their names to each other.
    "I'm Rose."
    "I'm Peony."
    "Did you hear . . . I'm called Zinia!"
    "Sweet Pea! That's ME!"
    "Daffodil! Jonquil!"
    "I'm Hyacinth!"
    "I'm called TUlips!"

Adam turned to go.

85

But still the little white flower had not been noticed.
It spoke so softly.
It was so pale.
Adam had not noticed it at all.

But now the flower got it's courage up.
It tugged at Adam's clothing.
It cried out as loud as it could.
"Adam! Forget-me-NOT!
Forget-me-NOT!"
Adam knelt to see this little flower.
A flower so bold it would speak like that to Adam.

"Why you are so small . . .
You're face is so pale . . .
I didn't see you waiting there at all."

Adam picked the little flower up and held it in his hands.
"You will not be overlooked again, little flower.
I cannot make you larger,
but I will turn your face as blue as the sky.
And your heart, I will make gold like the stars.
Wherever you grow, people will notice you.
And they will not forget YOUR name.
You will be called "Forget-me-not!"

And this is true.
The tiny Forget-me-not blossoms are such a bright blue that we notice
   them at once in our gardens.
And we never forget this flower's name.
We always run to see them calling "Oh, LOOK! Forget-me-nots!"

NOTES ON TELLING

It is fun to do a bit of acting with this story as you endow each flower with it's own personality. "I'm Rose!" "I'm Peony."

A display of flowers enhances the telling of this tale.

COMPARATIVE NOTES

Greatly expanded from a brief tale in Frances Olcott's *The Wonder Garden,* p. 38. Olcott calls it "a sweet old legend" but gives no source.

Stith Thompson's *Motif-Index of Folk-Literature* cites a Flemish source under A2657 *Origin of forget-me-not.*

I have elaborated considerably on the brief essence of the legend given in Olcott.

MAY DAY

May Day is the occasion for a spring outing in many European countries. Maypoles may be set up and colorful dances executed to wind them with ribbons. Flowers are gathered, and a May Queen may be crowned. A favorite May Day tradition in the United States and parts of Canada is the delivering of May baskets to friend's doorsteps. The baskets are made by children from brightly colored papers and filled with flowers from yard or field. The bearer usually hangs the basket on a friend's doorknob, rings the bell and runs. The door is opened to discover a cheerful basket of May flowers, with no donor in sight. In some areas these baskets are left mainly on the doorsteps of the elderly in the neighborhood. In other places they are left on the doorsteps of a would-be sweetheart. Nebraskans tell of filling their May baskets with popcorn! In the Indiana of my childhood they were always filled with wildflowers.

SUGGESTIONS FOR A MAY DAY CELEBRATION

Make May baskets of colorful paper. A very simple basket may be made by wrapping an $8^{1}/_{2} \times 11$ piece of paper into a funnel shape and stapling it in that shape. Staple on a strip of paper as a handle, and you have a basket.

A May Pole can be made from a freestanding classroom flagpole. Remove the flag.

Lay the pole on the floor and run a series of colorful crepe paper streamers up one side of the pole, across the top, and down the other side. Add enough streamers so that you have plenty of ends for your children to hold. I used twelve lengths of crepe paper (giving me twenty-four ends). Each streamer will be twice the length of the pole. Using plenty of strong tape, fasten this wad of crepe paper to the top of the flag pole. Stand the pole back up. Arrange the children in a circle around the flag pole. Pick up a crepe paper streamer end and present it to each child. Show the children how to let the paper drape prettily between their hand and the pole. If they hold it gently and refrain from pulling on the streamer it will not break. Circle the pole to wind it up, go back the other way to unwind it. Sing and dance as you do this:

"We're dancing round the May Pole, the May Pole, the May Pole. We're dancing round the May Pole on May Day."

FOR INFORMATION ON MAY DAY CUSTOMS IN MANY COUNTRIES

Folklore of World Holidays by Margaret Read MacDonald (Detroit: Gale Research, 1992), pp. 262–266.

FOR A SAMPLE MAY DAY PICTURE BOOK PROGRAM

Booksharing: 101 Programs for Preschoolers by Margaret Read MacDonald (Hamden, Conn.: Library Professional Publications, 1988), pp. 194–195. Includes music for the song given above.

TO SHARE WITH CHIDREN

Miss Flora McFlimsey's May Day by Mariana. (New York: Lothrop, Lee & Shepard, 1969). Miss Flora McFlimsey is made Queen of the May, after a day of helping her animal friends. Illustration too tiny to use with large groups. Could easily be adapted as a classroom May Day play.

THE SMALL YELLOW DRAGON

A Pai folktale from China.

In Yunnan Province, on the shores of Lake Erh, there once lived a
poor young woman.
She had been orphaned as a child, and she earned her living by
cutting grass for the horses of a wealthy family.
The young woman had built a little hut for herself and she lived there
all alone.
Sometimes the woman felt so alone.
She wished for a child to keep her company.

One day as she was cutting grass, she noticed something bobbing
along in the stream.

It looked like a green peach.

The girl fished it out of the stream and swallowed it.

Now the girl did not know this, but the green 'peach' was not a peach at all.

It was a dragon's egg!

Some time later the girl had a baby.

It was a most unusual child.

When the baby was born a huge Phoenix flew to the mother's small hut.

The Phoenix spread it's wings over the hut and protected the baby from the wind and the rain.

Later, when the mother took the baby to the fields with her, she made a little nest in the grass and tucked the baby into the grass, while she worked.

Whenever the baby cried, a large mother snake would crawl out of the bushes, coil around the baby and comfort him.

The young woman realized that her son was unusual.

By the time he was three years old he was able to walk along behind his mother in the field and help her cut grass.

By the time he was five years old he could read and write, and he could speak so persuasively that everyone who heard him was amazed.

Now at this time there lived in the waters of Lake Erh a huge Black Dragon.

The Black Dragon had gone beserk.

He would storm about the lake, creating such rough waters that the fisherman could no longer venture out to catch fish.

The people who lived on the shores of Lake Erh had no more fish to eat.

And to make matters worse, the Black Dragon had decided to dam up
the lake.
He had pushed huge boulders across the spot where the river ran out
of the lake.
Since the water could no longer run out through the river, the water
in the lake began to back up and the lake rose higher and higher.
Homes along the lakeshore were flooded and fields were covered with
water.

The Magistrate of the district posted signs calling for help in
controlling this Black Dragon.

One day the young woman's son went to town with his mother.
He read one of these posters on a wall.
"Mother, Mother, The Black Dragon is raging in Lake Erh.
The people have no fish to eat.
Mother, Mother, The Black Dragon has damned up the
lake.
The people's homes and fields are being drowned.
I must help them."

"But you are only a little boy, my son.
What do you think *you* can do?"

"Mother, I am young, but I can do some things.
Take me to the Magistrate."

His mother took the child to the Magistrate.
"This is my little son.
I know he looks small, but he is very unusual."
And she told the Magistrate about the Phoenix at his birth, and the
boy's unusual growth.

The boy spoke so persuasively that the Magistrate was impressed.

"But how can a small child like you hope to control a huge
dragon?"

"I can do it. But you will need to prepare some things to
help.
Can you do that?"

"What do you need?"

"I will need three large dragons woven of straw.
Can you make those?"

"Yes, we can make those."

"I will need 300 flour dumplings. Very tasty.
Can you do that?"

"Oh yes, we can do that."

"I will need 300 iron dumplings. Very heavy.
Can you do that?"

"Yes, the blacksmith can forge them for you."

"I will need something more.
I will need a little bronze dragon mask, just the right size
for me to wear.
I will need bronze dragon claws. One for each finger.
I will need six sharp swords.
And a yellow silk shirt to wear."

"We can prepare all of this."

"Then call me when it is ready."

The Magistrate ordered all of these things to be made.
When everything was ready, he sent for the little boy.
The little boy put on the yellow silk shirt.
He put on the bronze dragon mask.
He put on the bronze dragon claws.
Then he strapped four swords to his back,
and took a sword in each hand.

"I am ready.
Now . . . throw the first straw dragon into the water!"

The people pushed the large straw dragon into the lake.
Immediately, the huge Black Dragon emerged from the waters
    roaring.
"Enemy! Enemy!"
The Black Dragon attacked that straw figure.
He ripped and tore.
He rolled over and over in the water, wrestling with the straw dragon.
Until he had torn it to bits.
"I have VANQUISHED the ENEMY!"
He sank under the water again.

"Throw in the SECOND straw dragon!"

The people threw in the second straw dragon.
Immediately, the Black Dragon rose from the waters.
"Enemy! Enemy!"

He attacked that straw dragon.

He bit and tore.

He rolled over and over in the water, fighting that dragon.

Until he had torn it to bits.

      "I have VANQUISHED the ENEMY!"

The Black Dragon sank from sight.

      "Now the LAST straw dragon."

The people tossed the last straw dragon into the lake.

Up came the Black Dragon again.

      "Enemy! Enemy!"

He began to rip and tear.

He rolled over and over in the water, fighting that dragon.

Soon he had torn that straw dragon to bits also.

      "I have VANQUISHED the ENEMY!"

By now the Black Dragon was panting and wheezing from all of his
    exertion.

This fighting was starting to wear him out.

      "Now it is my turn." said the little boy.

To the people he gave instructions.

      "If you see yellow foam rise to the top of the water, throw
          in the flour dumplings.

      If you see black foam rise, throw in the iron dumplings.

      Will you do that?"

      "We will."

      "Then here I go."

The little boy JUMPED into the lake.

He sank slowly from sight.

The people stood in awe . . . waiting.

Then a whirlpool began to form in the water . . . faster and faster the
water swirled. . . .

and UP from the water rose a small yellow DRAGON.

That boy had turned into a DRAGON!

His little bronze mask had become a dragon head.

His bronze claws were now dragon claws.

On his back were four swords,

and in each hand a sword.

> "Come FIGHT, Black Dragon.
> Here is your REAL enemy!"

The Black Dragon rose roaring from the depths.

But before he could get his bearings, the Small Yellow Dragon had
begun to stab and slash at him.

The Small Yellow Dragon darted around and around the Black Dragon.

He was slashing here and stabbing there, while the huge Black
Dragon tried in vain to get a hold on him.

Then the two DID engage.

Rolling over and over they dissapeared under the waves.

The waters roiled.

The waters boiled.

Then yellow foam began to come to the top of the water.

> "Quick! Get the flour dumplings ready!"

The Small Yellow Dragon popped to the top of the water.

His mouth was open.

95

"Hungry! Hungry!
Food! Food!"
They tossed flour dumplings into his open mouth.
"MMM. MMM.
Strength! Strength!
Thank you! Thank you!"
And he sank beneath the waves again.

The water roiled and boiled.
Black foam came to the top of the water.

"Quick. Get the iron dumplings ready."

The Black Dragon rose to the top of the water.
"FOOD! FOOD!
HUNGRY! HUNGRY!"
He opened his huge mouth
and the people threw in the iron dumplings.
Those heavy iron dumplings sank to the dragon's stomach like rocks.
"HEAVY! HEAVY!
NOT food. NOT food."
The Black Dragon sank under the waves again.
The waters roiled and broiled.
Soon yellow foam floated to the top of the water once more.

"The flour dumplings! Get the flour dumplings ready!"

Up came the Small Yellow Dragon.
"Hungry! Hungry!
Food! Food!"
He opened his mouth and they tossed in flour dumplings.

"Strength! Strength!
Thank you! Thank you!"
The Small Yellow Dragon sank from sight.
The water roiled and boiled.
Soon *black* foam rose.

"Get the *iron* dumplings ready!"

Up rose the Black Dragon.
"HUNGRY! HUNGRY!
FOOD! FOOD!"
He opened his huge mouth and they threw in more iron dumplings.
"HEAVY! HEAVY!
NOT FOOD! NOT FOOD!"
The Black Dragon sank from sight.

For three days the fight continued.
Each time the Small Yellow Dragon rose, the people fed him with the
flour dumplings.
Each time the Black Dragon came up, the people tossed in more
dumplings of *iron.*
Eventually that Black Dragon's stomach became so full of heavy iron
that he could hardly move.
Still he dashed around with his mouth open . . . desperate for real
food.
"HUNGRY! HUNGRY!"

Then the Small Yellow Dragon saw his chance.
Holding tightly to his swords, the Small Yellow Dragon leaped into
the Black Dragon's mouth.
Down he slid into the Black Dragon's stomach, slashing all the time.

97

"Yeow! Yeow!" bellowed the Black Dragon.
"Get out of my STOMACH! Get out of my STOMACH!"

"If I come out, will you go away from Lake Erh and never
    return?"

"Yes Yes, Just come OUT of my STOMACH!"

"All right.
But how shall I come out."

"Come out through my mouth."

"You'd be sure to BITE me.
I won't do THAT."

"Come out through my intestines, then."

"Oh gross. I won't do THAT."

"Then come out through my ear."

"Yuck. I'd get ear wax all over.
I won't do THAT."

"Then come out through my nose.

"Ick. Too much snot.
I won't do THAT."

"Well, come out through my eye."

"Okay, take out your eye and I will come out."

So the Black Dragon removed one eye and the Small Yellow Dragon
  came out.
As soon as the Small Yellow Dragon was out of his body, the Black
  Dragon swam straight to the river that ran from Lake Erh.
He tore up the dam he had built and swam away down the river.
That Black Dragon never returned.

"I will stay and guard your beloved Lake Erh," said the
  Small Yellow Dragon.
"Mother come say goodbye to me, for I cannot go home
  with you again."
But when his mother came and saw her son with a *dragon* head the
  shock was so great that she keeled over and died.
"You must build a temple right here." said the Small Yellow
  Dragon, "and show honor to my mother.
I will remain in the lake and guard this place."

So the people brought stone and wood and built a temple for the
  Small Dragon's mother.
They called it 'The Temple of the Dragon's Mother'.
It is still there today on the shores of Lake Erh.
If you visit Yunnan Province and would like to see it,
just ask directions to The Temple of the Dragon's Mother.

And while you are there don't forget to pay your respects to The
  Small Yellow Dragon of the lake.

NOTES ON TELLING

The fight between the Black Dragon and the Small Yellow Dragon is very intense. I may repeat the episodes in which they rise to the top of the water and call for food several times. I ask the children to get their dumplings ready and we toss them into the mouth of the hungry dragon when it rises from the water.

Take time with the scene in which the boy puts on his armor and *becomes* a dragon. This is a magical moment.

If the "how should I come out" dialogue offends you, simply let the Black Dragon slink off in defeat and skip this episode.

The introductory set-up can be shortened for telling to younger audiences. The information about the dragon boy's birth, the phoenix, and the caregiving snake are interesting to older children but not vital to the plot. Younger children need to know only that this was an extraordinary little boy who grew rapidly and offered to fight the dragon. The child's request for dumplings and armor must be given in detail, however.

COMPARATIVE NOTES

Retold from "The Small Yellow Dragon and the Big Black Dragon: A Story of the Pai People" in *Folk Tales from China*. Fourth Series, pp. 79–87.

The story takes place at a village near Tali, in Yunnan province. I have adapted the story somewhat. The original makes much of the girl's unwanted pregnancy. In the actual ending, the people bury the mother and throw some grass onto the lake, the Yellow Dragon turns into a little snake, climbs onto the tuft of grass, and floats away with the current.

"The grass stopped drifting when it reached Fenglo Pavilion. Accordingly, the people built a Dragon King's temple nearby. They also erected a Dragon Mother's Ancestral Hall near the Three-Pagoda Temple. The Small Yellow Dragon was also worshipped as the local deity of Green Peach village."

The dragons in this story thrive on dumplings tossed into the water. See the legend of Ch'u Yuan, recounted below, for another dumpling-gobbling dragon.

The Dragon in Chinese lore is often associated with water, causing floods or bringing rains. Dragons may be either angry or beneficial. This tale includes Stith Thompson motifs B11.3.1.1 *Dragon lives in lake,* B11.7.2 *Dragon guards lake,* and B11.11 *Fight with dragon.* Motifs F912 *Victim kills swallower from within* and F914 *Person swallowed and disgorged* have many variants throughout the world. Stith Thompson lists African, Asian, European, Native American, and Oceanic variants as well as an early Babylonian source.

DOUBLE FIFTH: TUAN WU CHIEH/ DUAN WU JIE
A Chinese tradition

The fifth day of the fifth month is an inauspicious day in the Chinese year. Diseases and other dangers abound at this hot and sultry time of year. Precautions must be taken against the "five poisonous insects." The exact creatures named vary from area to area, and obviously not all are "insects." Scorpion, viper, centipede, house lizard, and spider are often named. In Taiwan wall-lizards, toads, centipedes, spiders, and snakes are named. The lizard which lives on the walls in tropical climates is not, in fact, poisonous at all, but folk tradition still names it as one of the "five poisonous insects" along with dangerous creatures such as scorpions and vipers. Cakes in the shape of these five creatures may be eaten to ward off their ills, small pieces of incense formed in the shape of the creatures may be worn around children's necks, or little cloth figures may be stuffed with incense. A variety of herbs may be burnt, hung up, or waved about on this day to help drive off the evils. Tigers may be embroidered on slippers or clothing to help scare off these creatures too.

Zhong Kui, the famous "Demon-Expelling General," is honored at this time. Zhong Kui appeared to the Tang Emperor Ming Huang (712–756) in a dream and explained that he had sworn to slay all demons in the other world to protect the emperor and his people.

Zhong Kui had committed suicide after failing the imperial examination because of his ugly appearance. Emperor Ming Huang, who was desperately ill at the time, recovered immediately after this dream. He ordered a picture of Zhong Kui painted after his dream, and Zhong Kui's tale is told to this day. Pictures of Zhong Kui gobbling up the "five ghosts" can be purchased at the time of the Double Fifth.

The Double Fifth celebration features dragon boat races. They are held in memory of a drowned third century B.C. minister Ch'u Yuan. Ch'u Yuan despaired for the fate of his country, and finding his advice rejected, he composed one last poem and threw himself into the river. His poem, one of the "Elegies of Ch'u" remains a classic of Chinese literature. People threw bamboo sections filled with rice into the river to honor his spirit. But Ch'u Yuan appeared to some fishermen, telling them that a river dragon was consuming the rice offerings meant for him. He instructed that the rice should be wrapped in small pieces of silk (some say chinaberry leaves) and tied with silk threads of five colors. These rice packets remain today as *zong zi*, sticky rice dumplings. They are wrapped in leaves, and made with a variety of fillings. This special treat is a favorite at Double Fifth.

It is said that when the people who lived by the Mi Lo river where Ch'u Yuan had thrown himself heard of his suicide, they paddled out to save him.

101

Failing this, they threw rice packages into the water for his spirit. From this legend comes the tradition of racing dragon boats. The prows of the boats are carved to represent dragons, and the rowing race is held amid much shouting and beating of gongs.

SUGGESTIONS FOR CELEBRATING DOUBLE FIFTH

Decorate the classroom or library with bright red streamers.

Tell "The Small Yellow Dragon".

Tell "The Little Rooster and the Heavenly Dragon", p. 1, which explains the cock's enmity with one of the five poisonous insects, the centipede.

Construct two large dragon heads from construction paper. Choose two dragon boat teams, let the leader carry the dragon head "prow" of the boat, or construct it as a helmet or mask so the leader can wear it. Paint two long boards bright red or decorate them with red construction paper. Each team member must hold onto his team's red board. Line up your dragon teams and let them race. For a version of this dragon race using ribbons intead of a board to form the dragon boat see p. 66 in *Venture Into Cultures*.

Make and eat cookies in the shape of the five poisonous insects.

Make small paper models of a dragon boat.

Snack on Chinese steamed buns or sticky rice cakes, or on traditional *zong zi,* if they are available.

See also the stories and activities for Chinese New Year in this book, p. 7.

FOR MORE INFORMATION ON DOUBLE FIFTH

"Double Fifth" in *Folklore of World Holidays* by Margaret Read MacDonald (Detroit: Gale Research, 1992), p. 310–314.

"Dragon Boat Festival" in *Fun with Chinese Festivals* by Tan Huay Peng. Illus. by Leong Kum Chuen (Union City, Calif.: Heian, 1991), p. 54–61.

"Dragon Boat Race" in *Venture Into Cultures: A Resource Book of Multicultural Materials & Programs*. Edited by Carla D. Hayden. (Chicago: American Library Association, 1992). Includes instructions for a dragon boat race on foot, and has excerpts from the final poem of Chu Yuan, the *Li Sao*.

BOOKS TO SHARE WITH CHILDREN

Eyes of the Dragon by Margaret Leaf. Illus. by Ed Young. (New York: Lothrop, Lee & Shepard Books, 1981). A dragon painting comes to life once its eyes are added. Read the comments on "painting a dragon" from the book's afterward and let the children paint their own dragon . . . with or without eyes.

Char Siu Bao Boy by Sandra S. Yamate. Illus. by Joyce M. W. Jenkin (Chicago: Polychrome, 1991). Charlie's friends make fun of his steamed bun lunches . . . until his grandmother makes enough for the whole class to taste.

LITTLE SNOT NOSE BOY

A tale from Japan.

In Japan there once lived a woodcutter so poor . . . so poor . . . that
    he had only a tiny wooden hut to live in.
Each day he climbed the mountain to cut wood.
Each evening he loaded the wood on his back and carried it down to
    the village to sell.
Down the mountain, with the heavy load on his back, across the high
    bridge over the sea, and into the village.

One evening no one would buy his wood.
He walked here and there looking for a buyer, but no one wanted
    wood that evening.

104

At last he turned to climb the hill to his little hut.

The wood was heavy on his back.

As he crossed the high bridge over the sea he had a thought.

"I believe I will give this load of wood to the Dragon King
as a gift.

Then it will at least do some good."

He lifted the wood from his back, held it over the water, and dropped
it into the sea.

He watched the heavy load disappear with a splash.

Suddenly he felt much better.

He had given someone a gift.

That always felt good.

Then he saw that the sea was starting to churn just at the spot where
he had dropped his wood.

As he stared in amazement a beautiful lady rose out of the sea!

She was holding a small boy in her arms.

"The Dragon King is pleased with your gift.

The Dragon Queen sends you this present."

She held out the little boy.

"Take good care of him and he will bring you luck."

The woodcutter reached down and took the little boy.

He held it out at arm's length.

He was bewildered

"What do I do with this . . . ?"

"There is just one thing.

You must feed him everyday with his favorite food . . .
shrimp sauce.

Do this and he will bring you great luck."

The beautiful lady vanished into the sea.

105

The woodcutter looked down at the child in his arms.
It was a fat little boy, but with SUCH a runny nose.
     "Yuck!"
The woodcutter hurried home, carrying the snot-nosed little boy in
     front of him.
His little hut was so bare he had only a single *zabuton* cushion to sit
     on.
The woodcutter sat the snot-nosed little boy on the zabuton.
The snot-nosed little boy began to snuffle and look around.
          "Now I have to feed it shrimp sauce," thought the
               woodcutter.
          "I don't even have money to buy rice for my own supper.
          Where will I get money to buy shrimp relish for this child."
Then he remembered that the beautiful lady had said the little boy
     would bring him luck.
He knelt on the floor in front of the zabuton and bowed politely.
          "Little Snot Nose Boy,
          The lady said you would bring me luck.
          I don't have any money to buy shrimp sauce for you.
          Do you think you could bring me good luck right now?"

The little snot nose boy looked up.
He stopped playing and shrugged.
Then "PFLUUUUG PFLUUUUG PFLUUUUG"
He blew his nose three times!

The woodcutter jumped back.
There on the floor was a huge pile of golden coins!
          "Thank you, Little Snot Nose Boy!
          Thank you, Little Snot Nose Boy!"

The woodcutter filled his pockets with money and ran to the market
place.
There he bought rice and fish for himself.
He bought shrimp sauce for the little snot nose boy.
He hurried home and prepared the shrimp sauce.
Then he placed a bowl before the little snot nose boy.
"Here. Shrimp sauce."
The little snot nose boy picked up the bowl.
"SLURRRP SLURRRP SLURRRP."
He swallowed it all down.
Then he set down the bowl and sighed.
"AAAAHHH!"

That night the woodcutter lay awake thinking.
"If that snot-nosed little kid can give me a pile of gold, I
wonder what ELSE he can give me?
What should I ask for tomorrow?"

The next day the woodcutter approached the little snot nose boy
again.
"The *gold* you gave me yesterday was really wonderful,
Little Snot Nose.
But I wonder if there is anything else you could give me.
The lady said you would bring me luck.
This house is pretty small.
Maybe a new house? A bigger one."

The little snot nose boy looked up.
He shrugged and
"PFLUUUG! PFLUUUUG! PFLUUUG!"
He blew his nose hard . . . three times.

Instantly . . . the wooducutter's hut vanished and an enormous
    mansion appeared.

"Thank you, Snot Nose Boy!
Thank you, Snot Nose Boy!"

The woodcutter was overjoyed!
He spent the day looking over his fine new home.
But in the evening he had to go down to the town and buy some
    shrimp sauce for the little snot nose boy.
"Here, Little Snot Nose.
Here is your supper."
The little snot nose boy picked up the bowl.
"SLURRP! SLURRP! SLURRP!"
He set down the bowl and sighed.
"AAAAHHH!"

Next morning the woodcutter had thought of *another* request for the
    snot nose boy.
"Dear Little Snot Nose Boy,
This new house is so marvelous.
But I really need servants to help keep it clean.
And some fine furniture would be useful . . .
And . . ."

The little snot nose boy shrugged.
He blew his nose hard . . . three times.
"PFLUUG! PFLUUG! PFLUUG!"
The door flew open and a row of servants marched in and bowed to
    their new master.
The woodcutter looked around and saw beautiful furnishing
    everywhere in his mansion.

"Thank you, Snot Nose Boy!
Thank you, Snot Nose Boy!"

That evening the woodcutter sent one of his servants to fetch the
shrimp sauce for the snot nose boy.
But the little snot nose refused to touch it.
So the woodcutter had to go buy some shrimp sauce and feed the snot
nose himself.
"Here, Little Snot Nose.
Here is your shrimp sauce."
The little snot nose boy picked up the bowl.
"SLURRP! SLURRP! SLURRP!"
He set down the bowl and sighed.
"Aaaahhhh!"

Each day the woodcutter thought of something else to ask of the snot-
nosed little boy.
Fine clothing. Jewels. A storehouse full of rich food. A stable of
horses. Even a beautiful wife.
Soon he had everything he could ever want.
He no longer went to the mountains to cut wood.
He stayed at home, waited on by his servants, pampered by his
beautiful wife.
He had riches enough to last a lifetime.
There was nothing more to ask of the snot-nosed little boy.
Still every day he had to go down to the market, buy shrimp sauce,
and feed the snot-nosed little child.
This became a real nuisance.
If anyone else brought the shrimp sauce the little snot nose would not
eat.
And the sight of that snot-nosed little kid really began to disgust him.

Now that he had everyting he could ever want, there was nothing
   more to ask.
What did he need this snot-nosed little brat for?
One day the woodcutter picked up the little snot nose boy and carried
   him out the front door.
He set him on the road and pointed toward the river.
      "You've done all the good you can do here," said the
         woodcutter.
      Go on back where you came from."

And the woodcutter went inside and shut the door behind him.

The little snot nose boy sat right down in the road.
He glared at that closed door.
He began to snuffle.
He snuffled and he snuffled.
Then he blew his nose HARD . . . three times.
      "PFLUUUUG! PFLUUUUG! PFLUUUUG!"

In an instant that door vanished.
That house vanished.
All of the gold, jewels, servants vanished.

The woodcutter was sitting on the floor in his tiny wooden hut.
His axe lay beside him.
Everything else had vanished.

He ran to the door, but there was no one there.
The little snot nose boy was gone.

NOTES ON TELLING

To carry this story well, the teller must be uninhibited by good taste. When Little
Snot Nose Boy blows his nose, I pinch my nose and make a guttural blowing noise

three times. I then deliberately pass my sleeve under my nose as if wiping off the snot. Left to right, then right to left.

After the first pile of gold, I let the audience suggest things the woodcutter might ask for. I usually let them suggest several items, then have the woodcutter ask for them all at once. They will usually ask for simple things like clothing and a new house at first. The next time I give them a chance to suggest things they become more elaborate . . . asking for sports cars, swimming pools, and other luxury items. I usually add in servants and sometimes a wife. If the audience suggests asking for shrimp sauce, I let the snot nose boy shake his head and refuse to grant that one thing. Then I explain that the woodcutter had to provide *that* himself.

COMPARATIVE NOTES

Retold from "The Little Boy from the Dragon Palace," (Shintoku Dōji or Nyoi Doji) in *Ancient Tales in Modern Japan: An Anthology of Japanese Folk Tales* by Fanny Hagin Mayer, pp. 90–91. The tale was collected from Mine Kosei, Tamana-gun, Kumamoto. It was translated from "Hanatare Kozo," pp. 7–20 in *Tabi to Densetsu II* by Masanori Hagiwara, ed., 1929.

A discussion of several Japanese variants of this tale appears in *The Japanese Psyche: Major Motifs in the Fairy Tales of Japan* by Hayao Kawai, translated by Hayao Kawai and Sachiko Reece. See "Hyōtoku," pp. 144–149. See also a variant from Iwate Prefecture (pp. 222–223). In this version the child has a mis-shappen face and keeps fiddling with his navel. Gold comes from the child's navel. The greedy old man's wife pokes the child's navel with a metal chopstick trying to get more gold and it dies. In a dream the child tells the old man to make a mask which looks like its misshappen face and hang this over the stove for luck. Such masks, called "Iron-Pot Man" became popular in the area. "Hyōtoku" means "fire blower", taken from the pursed lips of the mask.

The story reminds us of the many variants of J1415 *Foolish imitation of lucky man.* In many Japanese tales a greedy rich man imitates the luck bringing act of a kind poor man and is rewarded with bad luck. In our tale the poor man *becomes* the greedy rich man over time. The tale also utlizes Stith Thompson Motif W154.25 *Man demands ever larger gifts.*

BOY'S DAY, TANGO NO SEKKU
Japanese Tradition

On this day wind socks made in the shape of carp are flown from a bamboo pole set in front of the boy's house. One carp is attached for each boy in the household. The

111

oldest boy's largest carp flies from the top of the pole, with his siblings' smaller carp arranged in descending order of age/size below. Boys may arrange a display of military dolls on this day and friends may be invited to visit to admire the display and to taste iris-wine. The iris is thought of as a spiritual weapon, because its sword-like leafs are believed to deter evil spirits. These leaves can be added to one's bath on the fifth day of the fifth moon to prevent illness during the summer. The flower's petals can be added to sake to create a drink assuring longevity.

In 1948, May 5 was named Children's Day (Kodomo-no-hi) in Japan. Today activities for both boys and girls are held, though the theme of Tango No Sekku still dominates. In the United States the holiday is celebrated primarily as Tango No Sekku, a day for boys to celebrate. Girl's have their own day on March 3.

SUGGESTIONS FOR A BOY'S DAY CELEBRATION

Share stories about Japanese boy heroes such as Momotaro and Kintaro.

Make a paper carp wind sock:

1. Precut fish shapes from colored tissue paper. Cut two pieces at once.
2. Paste the edges of the two fish pieces together leaving an opening for the mouth.
3. Paint on scales, gills, and eyes.
4. Splash the fish gently with water or a solution of weak bleach or lemon juice. You can drop the liquid drops on the fish with a drinking straw. Dip the straw in the liquid, put your finger over the top of the straw, hold the straw over your fish and lift your finger . . . the water which was forced up into the straw by air pressure will drop out onto your fish making a splotch.
5. Cut a strip of stiff paper and fasten it into a roll to fit inside the fish mouth. Staple it and paste this stiff paper ring inside the fish mouth.
6. Fasten a string or ribbon to your fish's mouth and hang it in the breeze.

Make an iris picture. A handsome picture of an iris can be made using tempera paints. Spread plates with purple, green, and yellow tempera paints. Press the side of your hand into the green paint and draw an iris stem and two leaves using the side of your hand. Wash your hand. Press the side of both hands into the purple paint. Cupping your hands together make an imprint just above the green stem. This is the iris flower. Make an identical print upside down to form the lower part of the flower. Wash your hands. Using the tips of your fingers add three yellow dots in the heart of the iris.

FOR MORE INFORMATION

"Dolls' Day and Boys' Day" in *Festivals in Asia*. Sponsored by the Asian Cultural Centre for Unesco (Tokyo: Kodansha, 1975), pp. 23–30.

"Tango No Sekku (Boys' Day)" pp. 274–275 in *Folklore of World Holidays* by Margaret Read MacDonald (Detroit: Gale Research, 1992) and "Boys' Day" in *Folklore of American Holidays* by Hennig Cohen and Tristram Potter Coffin. (Detroit: Gale Research, 1991).

"Tango No Sekku" in *Matsuri! Festival! Japanese American Celebrations and Activities*. by Nancy K. Araki & Jane M. Horii (Union City, Ca.: Heian International, 1978). Historical background. Directions for an elaborate display with streamers, banners, carp wind socks, an origami iris, and a baker's dough armour set.

"Tango No Sekku" in *Festivals for You to Celebrate* by Susan Purdy (Philadelphia: J. B. Lippincott, 1969), p 153–156. Directions for paper carp.

BOOKS TO SHARE

A Carp for Kimiko by Virginia Kroll. Illus. by Catherine Roundtree. Watertown, Mass.: Charlesbridge, 1993. Kimiko wants a carp to fly like her brother.

The Inch Boy by Junko Morimoto (New York: Viking Kestrel, 1984).

Issun Boshi, the Inchling by Momoko Ishii. Trans. by Yone Mizuta. Illus. by Fuku Akino (New York: Walker, 1967).

Kintaro's Adventures and Other Japanese Children's Stories by Florence Sakade. Illus. by Yoshio Hayashi (Rutland, Vt.: Charles C. Tuttle, 1958).

Little One Inch by Barbara Brenner. Illus. by Fred Brenner (New York: Coward, McCann, & Geoghegan, 1977).

Momotaro. Paper Play Series #1. Educational Progress Corporation, 1970. Text. by Elizabeth Scofield. Art by Yoshisuke Kurasaki. A large-format pop-up book with accompanying tape, including musical background. Comes in a boxed set of four such books: "Little One-Inch," "Urashimo Taro," "The Grateful Badger," and "Momotaro." Hold the book on your lap and move the tabs to make Momotaro and his friends move as the tape recounts the story.

Momotaro: The Peach Boy by Linda Shute (New York: Lothrop, Lee & Shepard, 1986).

Peach Boy and Other Japanese Children's Favorite Stories by Florence Sakade. Illus. by Yoshisuke Kurosaki (Rutland, Vt.: Charles E. Tuttle, 1958, 1979.

Peachboy. Videotape. 20 min. Written by Eric Metanas. Told by Sigourney Weaver. Illus by Jeffrey Smith. Music by Ryuichi Sakamoto. Rabbit Ears, 1991. Iconographic animation.

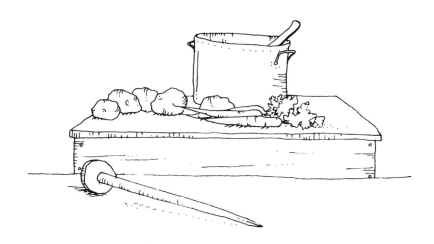

NAIL SOUP

A folktale from Norway.

An old woman lived all by herself in a little house by the edge of a
    fjord in Norway.
She was poor, but contented.
The woman had five little goats who grazed on the hillside behind her
    house.
Her house was built right up against the mountain and the grass grew
    down onto her rooftop.
So those little goats could graze on her roof!

She milked the goats every evening
and she drank some milk for her supper.

The rest of the milk she made into cheese to sell in town.
With the money from the cheese she could buy her supplies.
And of course she had a garden to grow vegetables,
so she lived quite well.

But one morning when the old woman woke up she didn't hear the
     little goats grazing on the roof.
She went outside and looked . . .
the goats were GONE!
They must have wandered off.
The old woman looked around her house.
She saw that her cupboards were bare!
She had one old meat bone.
She had one stale loaf of bread.
That was all!

The old woman went out and sat on her step and began to feel SO
     sorry for herself.
The sun was shining on the bright blue water in the fjord in front of
     her.
The hills were green behind her.
The sky was blue above her.
But she didn't see a bit of it.
          "Oooohhh what a miserable day.
          What a miserable, miserable day."
She fussed and fussed.

A young man was coming down the path.
          "Good day, old woman.
          Isn't this a gorgeous day today?"

          "It most certainly is NOT.

116

It is a *miserable* day.
A miserable, miserable day."

And she began to tell him her problems.
"My goats have run off
and now I won't have any milk for supper . . .
and no cheese to sell in the village . . .
and my cupboards are bare . . .
and I will probably STARVE!
. . . what a miserable, miserable day."

The young man said:
"Old Woman I will stay to lunch with you!
I will make you some of my excellent NAIL SOUP!"

"Nail Soup?
I never heard of nail soup.
How does one make soup from a nail?"

"Oh, it can be done.
But I will need your help."

So the Old Woman brought the young man into her house and he set
to work making the soup.
"I will need a large pot."
She brought him a pot.
"I will need water to fill it."
She went to the spring and brought back a bucket of clear cool water.
"That's good.
Now for the nail."
He took a nail from his pocket.
He dropped the nail into the soup with a "plunk"!

117

Then he built up the fire and the two sat back to wait for the soup to
 cook.
And while they waited, they chatted.
Good talk it was too, and soon the old woman was feeling some
 better.

"I will need a long-handled spoon to taste the soup."

"I have just the thing.
 Here is a long-handled wooden spoon which my husband
 carved for me when he was still living."
The young man took the long-handled spoon and began to stir the
 soup.
He stirrred . . .
and he stirred . . .
and he stirred . . .
and with a "SLU-U-U-RP"
and a "Smack-smack-smack-smack-smack"
he tasted it.
"Aaaahhhh . . .
Now THAT is good Nail Soup.

But . . . it does need a bit of salt.
I don't suppose you have any salt."

"Oh yes.
I'm sure I do."
The Old Woman opened her cupboard and brought out a paper
 wrapper with a bit of salt.
The young man dropped a pinchful into the soup.
Then he picked up the spoon.
And he stirred . . .

and he stirred . . .
and he stirred . . .
Then with a "SLU-U-U-RP"
and a "Smack-smack-smack-smack-smack"
he tasted it.

"Aaaahhhh . . .
Now THAT is good Nail Soup.

But it would taste even *better* if we had a bit of potato to
go in it.
I don't suppose you have a potato."

"You know, I *might* have.
There might be some potatoes left in the garden that I
missed when I dug them.
Shall I go look?"

"Go look."

She took her hoe and hoed all along the edge of the garden where her
potatoes had been planted . . .
and she found five small potatoes!

She washed them
and cut them up
and put them into the soup.

Then he stirred . . .
and he stirred . . .
and he stirred . . .
and with a "SL-U-U-U-RP"

and a "Smack-smack-smack-smack-smack"
he tasted it.

"Aaaahhhh . . .
Now THAT is good Nail Soup.

I don't suppose you would have a carrot to add to it.
A carrot would make it taste even better."

"I *might* have.
Let me go look in the garden.
Perhaps there is a carrot or two that I missed when I dug up
my carrots."
She went out and hoed all along where her carrots had been growing.
Sure enough, there were three little carrots!
She washed them
and cut them up
and put them into the soup.

He stirred it . . .
and he stirred it . . .
and he stirred it . . .
then with a "SLU-U-U-RP"
and a "Smack-smack-smack-smack-smack"
he tasted it.

"Aaaaahhhh . . .
Now THAT is good Nail Soup.

I don't suppose you'd have a bone to go in the soup.
That would help flavor it you know."

"Well yes, I do have a bone in the cupboard.
There's no meat on it though."

"Oh that doesn't matter.
It will do just fine to flavor the soup."

So they broke the bone and put it into the soup.

And he stirred . . .
and he stirred . . .
and he stirred . . .
then with a "SL-U-U-U-RP"
and a "Smack-smack-smack-smack-smack"
he tasted it.
"Aaaahhhh . . .
Now THAT is good Nail Soup.

I don't suppose you have a bit of bread to eat it with."

"I haven't a bit of bread in the house.
Except for an old stale loaf in the cupboard."

"Stale or fresh . . . it doesn't matter for soup!
We'll break it into the soup and it will be soft and soggy
    soon enough.
Bring it out!"

So the old woman brought out the hard loaf of bread and broke it in
    half. Half for the young man and half for herself.

"The soup must be almost ready!" said the young man.
So he stirred it . . .
and he stirred it . . .
and he stirred it . . .
and then with a "SLU-U-U-URP"

and a "Smack-smack-smack-smack-smack"
he tasted it.

"Aaaahhhh . . .
Now THAT is good Nail Soup!

And it is READY TO EAT!"

"Wait!" cried the Old Woman.
She ran to get a cloth for the table.
She set out a wooden bowl for the stranger
and a wooden bowl for herself.
She put down a pewter spoon for him
and a pewter spoon for herself.
She brought out a wooden mug for him
and a wooden mug for herself.
Then she ran to the spring for a fresh bucket of water
and filled his mug and her own with cool spring water.
"Now! We are ready to eat!"

Such a feast they had.
They broke the bread into the soup.
They stirred it around.
They tasted.

"Smack . . . smack . . . smack . . .
Smack . . . smack . . . smack . . .
Smack . . . smack . . . smack . . ."
Soon that delicious nail soup was all gone.

"Thank you for the fine lunch!" said the young man.
"I must be on my way now.
But I'd better take along my nail."

He took the nail from the pot, washed it off, and put it in his pocket.
"Good Day, Old Woman."
And he went whistling down the path.

As soon as he had gone,
the old woman looked around her house until she found a *nail*.
She put it in her pocket.
In case she wanted to make nail soup again some day.

Then she went out and sat on her front step.
She heard a sound.
Her little goats had come back and were grazing up on the roof
    again.
She looked at the blue waters of the fjord.
She looked at the green, green mountains.
She looked at the blue, blue sky.

"What a lovely day!" she said.
"What a lovely, lovely day!
Why didn't I notice it *before*."

NOTES ON TELLING

You may want to encourage your listeners to stir the soup with you. Then all dip up a spoonful and with a "Sluurrp" and a "Smack-smack-smack-smack-smack" give it a taste. End with a satisfied sigh, "Aaaahhhh".

Oline Heath's traveler offers to make her soup for "middag" (noon meal) and thanks her as he leaves saying "Mange tak for matten, god frau" (Many thanks for the food, good wife). If you have a Norwegian heritage in your family, you may want to add in a few such phrases as you tell the story.

It is fun to make soup while telling this story. In preschool storytime I handed each vegetable that was put into the soup to one of the mothers in attendance as I told the story. The mothers, who had been supplied with pans and paring knives, peeled and chopped and at the story's end we dumped all into our soup pot.

I had the water boiling already, and I had asked them to chop the vegetables very finely. So by the end of the storytime twenty minutes later, the soup was ready to eat. Older children can peel, chop, and make their own soup.

COMPARATIVE NOTES

This story is based on a version given to me by Oline Heath in 1989. Oline writes: "When I was growing up in a rural North Dakota community, my mother would sometimes give me a fifty-cent piece—one of those round, shiny, heavy, silver coins, embossed with Miss Liberty's head—and send me to the butcher shop to get "two pounds of beef off the shoulder," cautioning me to be sure to bring back ALL the change. (In those days that amount of meat cost about thirty-five cents.) There was no candy counter in the butcher shop, but I had been known to make a side trip on occasion. I would willingly run to do the errand, knowing that dinner would be our Dad's favorite meal: vegetable-beef soup with barley, and for dessert, either apple or lemon pie. For us kids, though, the biggest treat of all was the story we knew Dad would tell at meal time . . . the story about NAIL SOUP!"

Oline's father, Nicolai Ordahl, was born in Aardal in Jølster, Norway, in 1880. Oline writes "Jølster consists mainly of small, rocky farms lying between the glacier and Jølstervatnet, the fjord." Nicolai Ordahl must have been a fine storyteller, and his daughter's version bears many interesting touches sure to please children, such as the "slurp" and the "smack" at each tasting. Oline notes that these sound effects "were always very effective."

Interestingly, this variant goes beyond a simple trickster tale. The old woman (and the listener) learn that you can often make something out of nothing, if you change your outlook. As Oline tells it, the old woman seems not to be hiding her ingredients from the traveler, so much as just not realizing she has them.

Oline writes of the tale: "As a child, when I listened to this story, I always thought how clever the man had been to fool the woman into giving him all the ingredients for his soup; but there are some lessons here, too. First, things are usually not as bad as they seem. Second, no matter how little you think you have, there is always enough to share. And finally, sharing brings happiness to both giver and receiver."

This tale is Motif K112.2 *"Soup stone" wins hospitality. Tramp (soldier) makes stone soup (nail, hatchet) for hostess.* The tale appears in many adapations for children. Marcia Brown's *Stone Soup* presents a French variant in which a soldier makes soup with a stone. Harve and Margot Zemach's *Nail Soup* offers a Swedish variant (tramp uses nail). MacDonald's *Storyteller's Sourcebook* lists variants of this tale from Belgium, England, France, Russia, and Sweden. Aarne-Thompson's Type 1548 *The Soup-Stone Needs Only the Addition of a Few Vegetables* cites variants from England, France, Lithuania, Norway, Russia, Serbo-Croatia, Slovenia, and Sweden.

MIDSUMMER EVE: JONSOK/SAINT JOHN'S EVE. JUNE 23 EVE.
In the Norwegian tradition

The summer solstice, the longest day of the year, is greeted with celebration throughout Scandinavia. In Norway huge bonfires are lit beside lakes, rivers and fjords. Heaps of wood are collected for days . . . branches, tar barrels, fish crates . . . anything that will burn well. Everyone dances around the bonfire and eats and drinks long into the night. The dances continue without break, one musician replaces another, one dancer replaces another, as they dance on and on. Special activities for the children may be organized too, such as three legged races or sack races. A greased pole may be set up with a prize perched at the top. The older boys try to shinny up the greased pole to reach the prize. The sight of many bonfires burning on shores all along the fjords and bays makes this night seem magical. Boats decorated with greenery and flowers cruise the fjords taking in the sight of the sparkling bonfires and fireworks.

SUGGESTIONS FOR A CELEBRATION OF JONSOK

Decorate your space with garlands of greenery and flowers.

Learn a Norwegian dance. Try "Cut the Oats," a circle dance in *Children's Games from Many Lands* by Nina Millen (New York: Friendship Press, 1965), pp. 100–101.

Dance around a real bonfire outside or construct a fake bonfire inside to dance around.

Make your own open-face sandwiches. Provide several ingredients such as ham slices rolled up, baby shrimp, beef slices rolled up, cheeses, lettuce, thinly sliced cucumber, thinly sliced lemons, tomatoes. Each sandwich should contain a lettuce leaf, meat or cheese, and a cucumber or lemon garnish.

Eat up the "Nail Soup" you made during your story.

Snack on Norwegian cookies.

TO LEARN MORE ABOUT JONSOK

"Midsummer in the Land of the Midnight Sun" in *Holidays in Scandinavia* by Lee Wyndham (Champaign, Ill.: Garrard, 1975), pp. 52–63.

"Midsummer" in *Of Norwegian Ways* by Bent Vanberg. Illus. by Henning Jensen. (New York: Harper & Row, 1970), pp. 78–79.

RECIPES

"Open-face sandwiches/ Smørbrød" in *Cooking the Norwegian Way* by Sylvia Munsen (Minneapolis: Lerner, 1982), pp. 22–23.

Time Honored Norwegian Recipes by Sigrid Marstrander and Erma Olesan Van (Iowa City: Penfield Press, 1990. Includes cookie recipes and interesting recollections of turn of the century life in Norway and in Norwegian American homes.

PICTURE BOOKS TO SHARE

Springtime in Noisy Village by Astrid Lindgren. Illus. by Ilon Wiklund (New York: Viking, 1966). Springtime activities among children in neighboring Sweden, including dancing around a bonfire.

When the Sky Is Like Lace by Elinor Lander Horwitz. Illus. by Barbara Cooney (Philadelphia: Lippincott, 1979). Playful adventure on a moonlit night.

FOLKTALES TO SHARE

East of the Sun and West of the Moon by Peter Asbjørnsen and Jørgen Moe. Any edition. My favorite is *Norwegian Folktales* by Peter Christian Asbjørnsen and

Jørgen Moe. Illus. by Erik Werenskiold and Theodor Kittelsen (New York: Viking 1960). Asbjørnsen and Moe were early collectors of Norwegian folktales.

Midsummer Magic: A Garland of Stories, Charms and Recipes compiled by Ellin Greene. Illus. by Barbara Cooney (New York: Lothrop, Lee & Shepard, 1977). Folktales from around the world on a midsummer night theme.

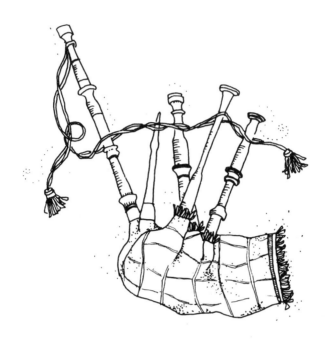

THE FINGER LOCK

A folktale from Scotland.

There were three McCrimmon brothers.
Handsome they were, all three.
But the elder two brothers ruled the lands
and left the younger brother to tend the sheep.

Now the older brothers had each a set of bagpipes,
and a fine kilt to wear when they played.
Each year when the Highland Games were held
those two brothers were there,
playing their pipes and winning the prizes.
But the younger brother was never allowed to go.

They left him at home in his raggedy clothes to sit and watch the
    sheep.

This summer as usual the brothers put on their fine kilts, took up
    their pipes and went off to the games.
They left the younger brother at home.
        "Stay out of the house while we're gone," they said.
        "Here's a crust of bread.
        That will do for your lunch.
        We're locking the house behind us."
And they locked the house and left.

The young brother sat on the hillside watching the sheep.
He dreamed of the Highland Games.
The bands would be piping now.
How he would like to hear them!
The lads and lassies would be dancing the fling . . .
Ah, that would be a sight to see.
And then the contest . . .
the *piping* contest.
That most of all he longed to hear.

Suddenly,
a little green man appeared beside him.
        "Now why are you looking so sad, my lad?" asked the little
            green man.
So the lad told him about the Highland Games that day.
And his own sad state left watching the sheep.
        "It's the piping I want to hear," said the lad.
        "How I would like to hear that music."

        "Well if it's piping you want,
        that I can give you." said the little green man.

And picking a straw from the ground,
he cut little holes in it and began to blow into it.
What music came from that tiny straw!
The lad sat entranced.
When the little man finished playing, he handed the straw to the lad.
    "Now you play a bit for me."

    "Oh I cannot play.
    My brothers have never allowed me to so much as touch
        their bagpipes.
    I can't even play the chanter."

    "Well that must *change*," said the little green man.
    "Let's take a look in the house and see what we can find."
    "I cannot go in the house," said the lad.
    "My brothers lock it when they are gone."

    "Oh that's no problem," said the little green man.
    "I'll show you a trick or two."
The little green man led him down to the house door.
    "Now *watch*," said the little green man.
He blew on his little finger . . . stuck it in the lock and turned . . .
    and the door fell open.
He pulled the door shut again.
    "Now *you* try it."
The lad blew on his little finger.
He stuck it into the lock.
He turned . . .
the door opened!

    "We'll, I never knew *that* trick!"
    "You do *now*."

The little green man led the way into the house.

"Now just open that old chest over there."

The lad looked.

There was an old dusty chest in the corner.

He never had noticed that chest before.

He pulled at the lid but it was locked.

"Don't forget what you've learned."

"Oh yes."

The lad blew on his little finger.

He stuck his finger in the lock and turned.

The trunk flew open.

Inside lay a *marvelous* set of bagpipes.

They were beautiful to behold.

He lifted them out and *under* them lay a handsome kilt.

It was woven of fine wool in the McCrimmon plaid!

The lad took it out and put it on.

There was a pair of stockings to match.

And a wee sporran purse to wear at his waist.

And a silver knife with a carved bone handle to wear in his stocking.

When the lad was dressed in all this finery he was fairly *dazzling* to
look at.

"Now play us a tune," said the wee man.

So he picked up the pipes.

He filled them with air.

And he began to play.

And he *could* play!

Such a *wonder.*

He played a tune he had heard his brothers play.

And fine it sounded.

"Not bad," said the wee man.

131

"But *here's* a tune for you.
Blow on your little finger
and see what we hear."

So the lad blew on his little finger and began to play again.
This time the tune that came from those pipes was so wonderful that
the lad himself nearly fainted from joy.
It was music such as had never been heard on this earth before that
time.
When he finished the lad had to set down and recover himself.
"What *was* that tune?" he asked.

"Let's call it the 'Finger Lock', " said the wee man.
"It's a tune I give just to *you*.
Now off to the games you must go."
When that lad arrived the crowd all turned to stare.
"Who is that handsome young man?"
"I've never seen him before."
"He's wearing McCrimmon plaid.
Is he related to you?" they asked the brothers.
But the two older brothers could not recognize him in his fine new
clothes.
"*We* don't know him, that's for sure."

When the piping contests began,
that lad took the stand.
He filled his pipes with air.
Then he blew on his little finger,
put his hand to the chanter
and he began to play.

Such music came from those bagpipes.

Never had the crowd heard a tune so wonderful.

They all stood back in awe.

>"What *was* that tune?"

>"Why the 'Finger Lock'," he said.

>"And now I must be going."

And without another word he whisked out of there and disappeared leaving them all in a wonder.

When the two brothers returned from the games that lad was sitting on the hill in his raggedy old clothes, watching the sheep.

>"What a time we had at the games," said his brothers.

>"There was a stranger there.

>Wearing McCrimmon plaid too.

>Though we can't think he is a relative of *ours*."

He played such a tune as has never been heard in this land before.

It was wondrous!

"What was the tune he played?" asked the younger brother.

"He called it the *FINGER LOCK*."

"Well I believe *I* know *that* tune."

And the younger brother went down to the house.

He blew on his little finger and the door flew open.

He went straight to the old trunk.

He took out the kilt and put it on.

He took out the stocking, the sporran, and the knife.

He took out the bagpipes.

Then he began to play.

He played the *Finger Lock*.

Those two brothers were *so* embarrased.

It was their own little brother who had won the crowd.

The one they had kept at home all these years . . .

he was the finest piper in all of Scotland.

From that day the two older brothers never went again to the
  Highland Games.
If there was piping to be held
at the Highland Games..
or at a Gathering of the Clan . . .
why it was the youngest lad who went.

And his piping made people glad throughout all of Scotland.

Now this is the story of the *origin* of that wonderful tune . . . *The
  Finger Lock.*

NOTES ON TELLING

I mime the action of blowing on my little finger and turning it in the lock each time
this occurs in the story. Usually the children silently perform this action too.

By all means bring along a tape of pipe music for the children to hear before
or after the story. It must be played loudly and should stir you to leap up and march
to the piping.

COMPARATIVE NOTES

Here is a male twist on the Cinderella motif (R221). A little green man provides
fine clothing and bagpipes for a trip to the Highland Games. Our hero wins no
bride, but does win the right to play his pipes and attend the games in the future.
The tale resembles R222 *Unkown knight (three day's tournament). For three days
in succession an unknown knight in different armour wins a tournament and es-
capes without recognition.* The story also includes Motif A1464.2.1 *Origin of
particular song.*

This tale is retold from "Finger Lock" in *A Dictionary of British Folk-
tales* by Katherine M. Briggs, Part A, V. I, pp. 234–237. It was collected by
Hamish Henderson of The School of Scottish Studies. The teller was Walter
Johnson.

HIGHLAND GAMES

A Scottish tradition.

Scottish communities celebrate in the summer months with a Gathering of the Clans and Highland Games. People of Scottish heritage have continued this tradition wherever they settled, so Highland Games are popular summer events in many areas of the United States, Canada, Australia, New Zealand, and in other countries. Wherever there are suffcient numbers of individuals of Scottish heritage to maintain piping and dancing schools, Highland Games are being held.

The event includes dancing competition in the Highland Fling, the Lilt, the Sword Dance, and other Scottish dances, all performed to the tune of a bagpiper. Piping and drumming competitions are held and entertainment is provided by marching pipe bands.The athletic games include tossing of the caber (a tree trunk around twenty feet long!), throwing the hammer (an iron ball on a chain), and putting the stone (a heavy stone thrown in shotput fashion). Hurdle jumping, footraces, and other athletic competitions may also be held. The tossing of the caber is the most exciting of the athletic events as the huge pole must be tossed so that it flips end over end.

SUGGESTIONS FOR CELEBRATING THE HIGHLAND GAMES

Talk about clan tartans and show a sample of tartan fabric.

Create your own tartan color combination. I provided a photocopied paper with bands drawn on as in tartan fabric. The children selected a color scheme and colored in the bands to create their own tartan pattern. Show sample tartans from a book such as *Scottish Clans & Tartans* by Ian Grimble (New York: Harmony Books, 1973).

Listen to pipe music. Form a marching band and march to the pipe music. Bring along a staff and take turns being the drum major and leading the band around.

Hold athletic contests in running, putting the stone, etc.

MORE ABOUT THE HIGHLAND GAMES

"Highland Games" in *The Customs and Ceremonies of Britain* by Charles Kightly (London: Thames & Hudson, 1986), pp. 137–139. Brief information on history and customs.

"Over the Sea to Scotland's Skye" in *The National Geographic Magazine*, July 1952, pp. 87–112.

BOOKS TO SHARE

Always Room For One More by Sorche Nic Leodhas. Illus. by Nonny Hogrogian (New York: Holt, Rinehart and Winston, 1965). Many folks, including pipers, crowd into this wee house.

All In the Morning Early by Sorche Nic Leodhas. Illus. by Evaline Ness (New York: Holt, Rinehart and Winston, 1963). Sandy goes to the mill for a sack of corn in this repetitive Scottish tale.

Wee Gillis by Munro Leaf (New York: Viking, 1938). This is the story of a boy who can't decide whether to live with his lowland relatives or his highland relatives. He becomes a piper and lives halfway between.

THE CLEVER DAUGHTER-IN-LAW

A folktale from China.

There once was a rich man who had three sons.

The two older sons were married and had chosen two lovely sisters as
brides.

The girls' father-in-law found both to be delightful company . . . and
they were a great help around the household. Soon he came to
depend on them very much.

But the two girls missed their mother.

Nearly every fortnight the girls would ask permission to go home and
visit their mother.

"Kind Father-in-law,

Would you give us permission to go home for a few days?
We would like to visit our mother."

The father-in-law always gave his permission, but he did not like to
have them leave his household so often.
He devised a plan to keep them from asking such a favor again, at
least for a while.

"I will suggest that they bring me back a gift the next time
they go to visit their mother.
Then I will name a gift so absurd that they will not possibly
be able to bring it.
They will be embarassed at not fufilling my request, and
will not ask ME for anything for some time."

He was pleased with his plan.
A few days later the girls came to him again.

"Kind Father-in-law,
Would you give us permission to go home for a few days?
We would like to visit our mother."
"Oh course," said the father-in-law.
But I would be glad if you would bring me back a gift
when you return."

"We would be pleased to bring you a gift, Dear Father-in-
law.
What would you like for us to bring you?"

"Something very simple, really," said the father-in-law.
He turned to the first daughter-in-law.

"I would like for *you* to bring me *wind*.
Wind wrapped in paper."
He turned to the second daughter-in-law.

"And I would like for *you* to bring me *fire*.
Fire wrapped in paper."

The girls were aghast.
Whatever could he mean by such a thing.
And however could they find gifts like this.
> "Wind wrapped in paper?" This was absurd.
> "Fire wrapped in paper?" The fire would surely burn the
> paper.
This was impossible.
The girls set out for their mother's village.
They were so upset by their father-in-law's request that they soon sat
down under a tree and began to weep.
> "We will not be able to bring our father-in-law the gifts he
> has asked of us.
> And if we do not give him the gifts he requests, we will be
> too embarassed to ever ask a favor of *him* again.
> What shall we do?"

A young girl who herded the water buffalo was passing by.
She saw these two girls weeping.
> "Whatever can be wrong?
> What makes you so miserable?"
They told the buffalo girl about their troubles.
She laughed.
> "Is that *all?*
> I can bring you wind in paper.
> I can bring you fire in paper.
> That is a *simple* thing.
> Come by here when you return from your mother's house
> and I will have the gifts ready for you.

But I will need a few coins to buy paper with,
I am just a peasant girl, you know."

They gave her some coins to buy paper and went on their way much
relieved.

When the two girls returned the next day the buffalo girl was waiting
for them.

"You wanted 'wind wrapped in paper'?
Here it is!"

The girl held up a paper fan.

She waved it and the wind moved before it.

"How clever!
Why didn't WE think of that!"

"And you wanted 'fire wrapped in paper'?
Here you have it!"

She held up a paper lantern.

The girl lit the candle inside the lantern . . . and . . .

FIRE wrapped in paper!

"How brilliant!
We never would have thought of that!"

They thanked the buffalo girl and hurried to their father-in-law with
the gifts.

When he saw them coming he began at once to gloat.

"Well it is too bad you didn't bring the gifts I asked.
I guess you will not be asking ME for favors in the future."

But the elder daughter-in-law said,

"Oh no. We have your gifts right here.

You asked for 'wind . . . wrapped in paper'?
Here it is!"
And she held up the fan.
She waved it back and forth and the wind swept through the room.
The father-in-law was amazed.
"How VERY clever!
I didn't imagine you would think of such a thing!"

The second daughter-in-law stepped forward.
"And HERE is your 'fire wrapped in paper."
She pulled out the paper lantern and lit the candle.
"FIRE . . . wrapped in paper."

The father-in-law could not believe this was possible.
"However did you THINK of these things?
I did not realize you were so clever."

"Oh we AREN'T.
It was the girl who tends the water buffallo.
She thought of this and made these gifts for us.
She is VERY clever!"

"Then I would like to meet this clever girl.
Invite her to our home."

When the girl came before the rich man he spoke to her for a long
time.
He saw at once how very clever she was.
"Would you like to work for our household?" he asked.
"We could use someone with brains like yours here.
I would like to get to know you better.

And I happen to have a younger son who is still unmarried.
Perhaps HE would like to get to know you too."

And do you know what happened after a while?
The younger son DID get to know her better.
And she got to know HIM better too.
In fact they were . . . MARRIED.

Now the father was delighted to have such a clever daughter-in-law.
He put her in charge of the entire household and made this young girl
    HEAD OF THE FAMILY.
She ran things so well that the estate began to prosper.
She spoke to all of the workers.
       "Whenever you go out to the fields . . . carry something
          with you.
       Whenever you come back from the fields . . . carry
          something with you."
So the workers always carried seed, or plants, or tools when they
    went to the fields.
And when they returned they always brought wood, or carried a
    stone.
Soon the stones had been cleared away from the fields, the fields had
    been planted and tilled, and enough wood had been gathered for
    the winter months.
In a few years the estate was so wealthy that the father-in-law built a
    new ancestral hall. Over the door he wrote the words "No
    sorrow." He wrote this up as a motto because the clever girl
    governed his household so well that they wanted for nothing.

Now one day the Mandarin who ruled that province was passing with
    his retinue.
He saw the motto "No sorrow" over the door.

142

"How IMPUDENT!

Who would put up such a sign?

Does the owner of this house think he is better than anyone
else?

Call him out. I want that sign removed at once!"

When the father-in-law had been called out he said,

"Your Honor, this is true.

My clever daughter-in-law governs our household so well
that we are without sorrow."

"Bring me this girl.

I want to see just how clever she is!"

The daughter-in-law came out.

"Young woman since you are so very clever I will set you a
task.

Before morning I want you to spin for me a piece of silk."

"Yes . . . your honor . . ."

". . . .I have not finished.

A piece of silk that is as long as this road."

The road stretched away out of the village, over the hills, into the
distance.

This was an impossible task.

The clever girl did not even blink in dismay.

"Your Honor.

I will start at once.

But you must tell me, exactly how long is this road?"

The Mandarin had no idea how long the road might be.

It stretched away beyond sight, into the next country even.

He saw that he was bested at this task.

"Never mind.

143

Forget about the silk.
I will set you another task.

From beans you must press oil for me."

"I will be glad to press oil for you."
". . . I am not finished.
You must press enough oil to equal the water in the Western
    Sea."

"Yes, Your Honor.
I will start at once.
But first tell me . . . exactly how much water is there in the
    Western Sea?"

Oh course no one could know the answer to such a thing.
The Mandarin was bested again.

"Never mind about the oil.
I will propose a riddle instead."

The Mandarin called one of his servants and took from him a bird
    cage.
In the cage was a small songbird.
The Mandarin removed the tiny bird and held it hidden in his hand.
    "Tell me.
    Do I plan to kill this bird?
    Or do I plan to set it free?"

    "Your Honor, this is a troubling question.
    If I answer that you plan to set the bird free, you can crush
        it in your hand and kill it.

144

> If I answer that you plan to kill the bird, you can open your
> hand and set it free.
> I am only a poor peasant girl.
> I cannot read the mind of one so great as you.
>
> But YOU who are a powerful Mandarin in this province,
> You can surely read MY mind.
> I stand here on the threshold of my house.
> One foot is in the yard, yet one foot remains in the house.
> Tell me, rich and mighty lord,
> Do I plan to go OUT of my house?
> Or do I plan to go IN again."

The Mandarin saw that he was bested yet a third time.

> "This girl is TRULY clever as you say.
> You can keep the sign above your door.
> Certainly a house which is governed by such a clever girl IS
> a house of little sorrow."

This is the story of the Clever Girl.

I wonder. . . .

What would she have said if she had been asked to bring *water* in
paper?

NOTES ON TELLING

You might want to have a paper fan and paper lantern hidden and produce them at
the appropriate moment in the story. At the story's end the audience likes to suggest
ways in which the young girl could have brought water wrapped in paper. A simple
folded paper cup is one obvious answer.

COMPARATIVE NOTES

MacDonald's *Storyteller's Sourcebook* lists six sources for this Chinese tale under
Motif H506.12 *Test: bring wind in paper and fire in paper. Daughter-in-law buys
fan and paper lantern.*

For other versions of this story see "The Young Head of the Cheng Family," pp. 25–33 in *Tales the People Tell in China* by Robert Wyndham; "The Young Head of the Family," pp. 259–264 in *The Fairy Ring* by Kate Douglas Wiggin, and "The Young Head of the Family" in *Wise Women: Folk and Fairy Tales from Around the World* by Suzanne Barchers.

MID-AUTUMN FEAST/CHUNG CH'IU/ TIONG-CHHIU/ZHONG QIU JIE

A Chinese tradition.

The mid-autumn feast is held on day fifteen, the full-moon day of the eighth moon. Chang-E (Heng-O), the Goddess of the Moon, is honored on this day.

In the evening everyone goes out to view the full moon. A special feast featuring round fruits may be layed out to honor the round full moon. Apples, oranges, peaches, and pomegranates may be served. Special moon-cake treats are eaten. A traditional moon cake may be shaped like a drum the size of a small saucer. It is filled with lotus seeds or a red bean paste and melon seeds. A salted duck's egg yolk, symbolizing the moon, forms the center. Small candle-lit lanterns are taken to the picnic grounds and families spread their parties out and sit to watch the moon rise.

In some areas a children's lantern parade is held on this night as well as during the Lantern Festival of the New Year celebration.

The story of Chang E, who married the miraculous archer Hou Yi, is recalled at this time. Hou Yi managed to shoot out nine of the ten suns plaguing the earth in those days, leaving only one . . . providing just the right amount of heat. The Queen Mother of the West, Xi Wang Mu, rewarded him with a pill of immortality. Chang E, however, discovered the pill and swallowed it herself. Amazingly she could now fly. In panic she fled from her angry husband, flying all the way to the moon. There she spit out the pill's casing . . . which turned into a jade rabbit. She herself turned into a three-legged toad. Both can be seen on the moon to this day. Hou Yi built himself a palace on the sun and the two see each other on the fifteenth day of each month.

SUGGESTIONS FOR CELEBRATING THE MID-AUTUMN FEAST

Prepare a feast table with round fruits to dine on.
Bake round moon cakes or round almond cookies.

Arrange for an evening outing to view the full moon.
Bring along round fruits and round cakes or cookies to share.

Make a lantern to carry and hang it from a wooden stick (see illustration above).
Have a lantern parade.

Read or tell the story of Chang-E. A good version is found as "Heng-O, the Moon Lady" in *Tales of a Chinese Grandmother.*

SUGGESTION: These activities could be used also to celebrate the "Lantern Festival" which ends the New Year Celebrations on the fifteenth day of Moon One. You might want to carry out these festivities at the full moon of Moon Nine or Ten rather than at the traditional time, since Moon Eight may fall too early in the school year to prepare a moon watching excursion.

FOR MORE INFORMATION ON THE MID AUTUMN FESTIVAL

"Mid-Autumn Feast/Chung Ch'Iu/Chusok/Tiong-Chhiu Choeh/Trung Thu" in *Folklore of World Holidays* by Margaret Read MacDonald (Detroit: Gale Research, 1992), pp. 428–432.

"Mid-Autumn Festival" in *Chinese Festivals* by Tan Huay Peng. Illus. by Leong Kum Chuen (Union City, Calif.: Heian International, 1991), pp. 76–83.

TO SHARE

"Heng O, the Moon Lady" in *Tales of a Chinese Grandmother* by Frances Carpenter (New York: Doubleday, 1937), pp. 206–216.

The Moon Lady by Amy Tan. Illus. by Gretchen Shields (New York: MacMillan, 1992). Illustrated story of a grandmother's adventures on the night of the moon festival long ago, when she was a little girl in China.

"The Secret of the Moon Cake," in *Traditional Chinese Folktales* by Yin-lien C. Chin, Yetta S. Center, and Mildred Ross (Armonk, N.Y.: M.E. Sharpe, 1989), pp. 171–180. Fictionalized account of supposed historic event in which messages were hidden in moon cakes under the eyes of invading Mongols.

STINKY SPIRITS

An Igbo folktale from Nigeria.

There was a man who had two wives.
The senior wife had many children.
But the younger wife had only one child, a son.
This family had a field which was far away.
It lay right at the boundary between the land of men and the land of
   the spirits.

In the daytime it was safe to work in this field.
But as soon as it became dark, the spirits came out of the forest.
After dark the field belonged to them.

149

When there was work to be done in this far field, the family left
   home early in the morning carrying their hoes and baskets.

They crossed seven streams.
They passed through seven wilds.
They came to their field
and they worked all day planting yams.
At noontime they stopped to rest.

The son of the younger wife took out his bamboo flute and began to
   play.
            "This is our field
            We will work hard.
            This is our field
            where yams will grow."

That is the song he played.

When the sun began to go down the family gathered up their hoes
   and baskets and started the long walk home.

They crossed seven streams.
They passed through seven wilds.
They reached their home.

But what bad luck!
The son of the youngest wife had left his bamboo flute behind in the
   field.

            "You cannot go back now," said his father.
            "The spirits will be in the field by now.
            If you go, you might die."

"Do not go back," said his mother.
"You can go find your flute in the morning."

But boy would not listen.
He would not leave his bamboo flute lying alone in the grasses during
    the dark night and the damp dew.
So he set out.

That boy crossed seven streams.
That boy passed through seven wilds.
He came to the yam field.

The spirits were already there.
They were moving all over that field.
They were planting their ghost-yams.

      "Taaaa! A human boy!", whined the spirit leader.
      "This is the time of the spirits!
      Humans are not allowed!"

The spirit talked through his nose.
That is the way with spirits.

Now these spirits were very ugly.
And they smelled just awful.

But the boy did not forget his manners.
      "Pardon me for bothering you.
      I . . . forgot my flute.
      Please may I go get it?
      I left it under that tree on the other side of the field."

"We have found a flute.
Will you recognize your flute if you see it?"

"Oh yes."

"Is THIS your flute?" The spirit leader held up a flute of
shining yellow metal. It was solid GOLD!

That golden flute was so beautiful.
The boy wished it could be his own.
But he was an honest boy.

"No. That is not my flute. Somone else must have lost that
flute."

The spirits muttered among themselves.

Then the leader held up a flute that was shining white like the nut of
the water of heaven. It was made of SILVER!

"If this your flute?"

"No. That is not my flute."

The spirit held up a flute of bamboo. It was old and scarred.

"Is this your flute?"

"Yes. THAT is my own flute!"

"Then take it and play for us."

152

The boy took the flute from the hand of the spirit.
He began to play.

> "Awesome Spirit, this is your land
> through the dark, the long dark night.
>
> Mother told me, 'Wait till morning.'
> Father told me 'Death is there.'
>
> But I could not sleep till dawn
> leave my flute forgotten here
> lying in the damp and dew."

The spirits were delighted with the boy's song.
They began to laugh approvingly, haw-haw-hawing through their
     noses and shaking their heads from side to side.

> "Haw . . . haw . . . haw . . . haw . . . haw . . .
> This boy pleases us."

The spirit leader brought out two pots.
These pots were sealed.
> "You may take one of these as a gift from the spirits."

The boy looked at the pots.
He did not want to seem greedy.
He chose the smaller pot.
> "Aaaahhhh. Aaaahhh." The spirits were pleased.
> "When you reach home, call your mother and your father.
> Break the pot in front of them."

The boy thanked the spirits for their gift and started home.

That boy crossed seven streams.
That boy passed seven wilds.

When he reached his home the boy called his mother and father.
He broke the pot in front of them.

Then from the pot poured every good thing imaginable!
Gold, fine cloths, velvets, excellent foods, even cows and goats
    spilled out of that magic pot.

The boy's mother was so pleased, she wanted to share this good
    fortune.
She prepared a basket filled with these good things and sent it as a
    gift to the senior wife's house.

When that woman saw these riches she was jealous.
And when she heard how they had been obtained she began to
    scheme.

Next day the senior wife called her oldest son.
        "Bring your flute.
        We are going to the distant yam field."

They crossed seven streams.
They passed seven wilds.
They came to the yam field.

But they did not care to work.
They sat in the shade all day.

When the sun began to set the senior wife said to her son.
        "Come, we can go home now."

154

Her son picked up his flute to go.
That mother whacked him on the head.

> "Foolish boy!
> Don't you even know how to forget your flute!"

So the boy dropped the flute in the grass and followed his mother
home.
When they had passed the seven streams and the seven wilds the
mother turned to her son.

> "Now go back.
> Get your flute."

The boy began to cry.
He was afraid.
He knew what horrid spirits came to that field at night.

But his mother would not listen.
So the boy set out again for the field.

He crossed the seven streams.
He passed the seven wilds.

When he came to the field the spirits were already going about their
planting.

They were so ugly.
And they did STINK.

That boy had no manners whatsoever.

> "PHEW! PHEW! I am choking with the stink of these
> spirits," he complained.

The king of the spirits looked up.

155

"Is this another human boy?
What have you come for?"

"My mother sent me back to get my flute.
Phew! Phew! You stink!"

The spirit ignored the boy's rude comments.
"Would you recognize your flute if you saw it?"

"What a stupid question. Of course I would.
Phew! Phew! What a smell!"

"Well, is this your flute?" The spirit held up a flute shining
like yellow metal. It was the flute of solid gold.

"That's it! Of course that's mine!" shouted the greedy boy.

"Then take it and play for us." said the spirit.

The boy took the flute from the spirit's hand.
"Yuck, yuck. I hope you haven't been spitting in it!"
The boy wiped the flute mouth clean.
Then he began to play.
"King of Spirits. He stinks!
Phew! Phew!
Old Spirit. He stinks!
Phew! Phew!
Young Spirit. He stinks!
Phew! Phew!
Mother Spirit. She stinks!
Phew! Phew!

Father Spirit. He stinks too!
Phew! Phew!"
When he finished playing, the spirits were all silent.
Then the leader brought out two pots.
One was large. One was small.
"You may choose one of these . . ."
Before he had even finished speaking the boy had grabbed the largest
pot and was running back toward his village.
The boy did not even thank the spirits.
He just took his prize and ran.

The boy crossed seven streams.
He passed seven wilds.
He reached his home.

"Come quick," said his mother.
"Let's break the pot!"

She stopped up all of the cracks in her wall and shut tight her door so
none of the spirit gifts could escape.
Then she smashed that pot.

Things began to spill from the pot.
But they were not good things.
Sickness began to crawl from the pot.
Diseases of every kind crept out.
Leprosy . . . smallpox . . . yaws . . .
and diseases so horrible they have no name.

All flowed from the pot and surrounded the woman and her son.
Death came to both.

157

In the morning her husband, seeing that no one was stirring in that house, pushed the door open a crack.

Diseases began to pour from the door!

Struggling against them the husband managed to get the door shut. But already many diseases had escaped and were spreading throughout the world.

Fortunately the worst of them, those without a name, still remained trapped in that house.

Sometimes a stranger will pass by that village and seeing this old locked up house will just peep in the door. Then more diseases sneak out. And men must work hard to learn their names and defeat them.

Now this is important.

If you ever pass through that village and you see an old abandonned house with the door shut tight. . . .do NOT open that door.

NOTES ON TELLING

Create a tune to sing as the son plays on his flute. If you can play a simple tune on a small wooden flute, by all means do so. Inexpensive bamboo flutes are often available in import shops.

The Stinky Spirits talk through their noses in a whining nasal tone. Work on their voice until you get it just right. Of course the wicked boy is holding his nose and wrinkling up his face in disgust as he sings of the Stinky Spirits.

COMPARATIVE NOTES

This story is retold from a Nigerian folktale related in *Arrow of God* by Chinua Achebe. Acebe's tale contains an interesting bit which I have left out of my telling.

You might like to include it. When the spirits send the good boy home they tell him "If you hear 'jam jam' jump into the bush. If you hear 'dum dum' come out again." He hears these sounds on the way home and obeys. The wicked boy hears them and does the opposite of his instructions.

This is Stith Thompson Motif Q3.1 *Woodsman and the gold axe. A woodsman lets his axe fall into the water. Hermes comes to his rescue. Takes out a gold axe but the woodsman says that it is not his. The same with a silver axe. Finally he is given his own axe and rewarded for his modest choice. His companion tries this plan and loses his axe.* Thompson lists Lituanian, Chinese, and Japanese variants as well as the Aesop tale described. MacDonald's *Storyteller's Sourcebook* gives sources from Russia, Japan, and Aesop.

YAM FESTIVAL

To many West African cultures the yam is a primary food. The harvesting of the first yams of the season is a ceremonial event. In most Nigerian cultures the time of the digging of the first yam must be set by community's religious leaders and must be carried out exactly according to tradition. After the priests have performed the proper rituals and offered a taste of the new yam harvest to the deities, the community erupts into a joyful celebration of the new harvest. The digging of the yams ushers in a time of plenty. This is a time for dancing, singing, and partying into the night. Yam *fufu* is a popular dish in many areas.

In Ghana the Akan celebrate with their Odwira festival. The Akan calendar consists of forty day cycles. A religious ceremony, the Adae, is held every forty days. Odwira takes place at the time of the ninth Adae of the year. This traditionally falls between August and October but in recent years the celebration has been moved to the drier period between November and January in some areas. According to legend the first yam was discovered by a hunter in the bush. He brought it home and later noticed an animal eating on it. He told the Chief of Guendé and the chief had the yam cooked and ate it. The people waited forty days and nights. When the chief did not die they knew that yam was good to eat. Each year this event is re-enacted at Guendé as the Chief of Guendé eats a yam before the King.

Traditions vary from area to area. In Peki in the Volta region, the Yam Festival occurs on a Friday. On Tuesday the town is cleaned thoroughly, the streets are swept and weeded and each home is cleaned. After sunset every fire is put out and each fireplace is cleaned. All of the ashes from the community fireplaces are piled in a single heap in the middle of the village road. The priest and the village men process through the streets and ritually mark this spot to prevent evil from entering the town. On Thursday the first yams are dug from the fields. They are hidden in the bushes and carried into the town amid singing from dusk to 8 P.M. on Thursday and from dawn to 8 A.M. on Friday. Onlookers run after the farmers and pound the yams they like gently with their fists, while singing songs about the new yam harvest. On Friday the chief of each Peki town sends to the chief priest a chicken and two yams. The priest prepares a special yam *fufu* meal from these. Plain yam and red yam (mixed with palm oil) are sprinkled on the shrine for the ancestral spirits to partake. The chief cuts the head from a yam and places it in a mound in a corner of the shrine where it will sprout and become the first yam of the next growing season.

People visit their friends on this day and wish each other a good new year. Prize yams are displayed at each house. Everyone feasts on *fufu* and a soup prepared with chicken, goat, or smoked river fish. Children play with tops, toss palm leaf bundles, and compete at somersaulting. Dancing, drumming, and singing occupy everyone. The festival lasts for a week. On the following Thursday just after dusk a male of each household takes a brand from the fireplace and waves it over every corner of the house to drive off evil spirits. He then races out of town with a shout and tosses the brand into the tallest tree he can find. This ends the festival.

Not all African cultures celebrate the yam. Some cultures depend more on millet, corn, or rice for their staple. In those cultures the harvest festival praises that important crop.

SUGGESTIONS FOR A YAM FESTIVAL CELEBRATION

Decorate your space with harvest colors and harvest fruits from your area . . . corn, pumpkins, squash. Also arrange a display of yams of several sizes and shapes.

Have a yam contest. Divide the children into four teams. Let each child select a favorite yam from your pile. One by one each team should leave the room and run back in holding up their yams and singing about how great these yams are. Let each team make up their own yam song. The onlookers can vote on their favorite yam from those displayed by going up to the yam holders and pounding gently on that yam with their fists. The yam with the most votes is set in a special place. Repeat with each team until you have four yams chosen. Each person in the room can then vote for their favorite yam by pounding gently on that yam with a fist. Award that yam a prize ribbon.

Make *fufu* and share it. Peel your sweet potatoes and boil them until soft. Mash them well. Roll the mashed sweet potatoes into balls. Laurens Van Der Post's *African Cooking* (New York: Time-Life, 1970, p. 70) suggests rolling the yam balls on a dampened plate to round them. Instructions also appear as "From Ghana: Fufu" in *Many Hands Cooking: An International Cookbook for Boys and Girls* by Terry Touff Cooper and Marilyn Ratner. Illus. Tony Chen. (New York: Thomas Y. Crowell in cooperation with UNICEF, 1974, p. 13).

Make a sweet potato cutting. Choose a sweet potato with several eyes. Suspend it in a glass of water by sticking a toothpick into each side of the potato and resting these on the rim of the glass. Half of the potato should be underwater. Sprouts will form from the eyes in about two weeks, then leaves and a vine will follow.

FOR MORE INFORMATION ON HARVEST FESTIVALS

"Harvest Festivals" in *Folklore of World Holidays* by Margaret Read MacDonald (Detroit: Gale Research, 1992), pp. 444–470.

"Ghana and Togo," "Liberia," "Nigeria" in *Children's Games from Many Lands,* by Nina Millen. (New York: Friendship Press, 1964), pp. 28–29, 32–34.

For your own education you might like to read the adult novel *Arrow of God* by Chinua Achebe (New York: John Day, 1967). The story revolves around the dilemna of an Ibo priest who cannot bring himself to announce the start of the New Yam festival.

BOOKS TO SHARE

MA nDA LA by Arnold Adoff. Illus. by Emily McCully. (New York: Harper & Row, 1971). An African family harvests corn.

SPARROW'S LUCK!

A folktale from India.

Little sparrow lived with an old, old woman.
He called her his "granny".
One day as sparrow was hopping about in the courtyard
he found a tiny grain of rice.

> "Sparrow's LUCK!
> Sparrow's LUCK!" he began to chirp.
> "This grain of rice is MINE.
> What LUCK!"

Sparrow flew straight to Granny and asked her to keep his grain of
rice for him.

> "Put it up on the shelf so you don't loose it."

Granny humored him.

> "Oh, yes, yes, little sparrow.
>
> I will take good care of your grain of rice."

She put the rice up on a high shelf and little sparrow went out to peck in the courtyard.

But when Granny began cleaning her house she *forgot* about that grain of rice and dusted it right off the shelf.

Later sparrow returned.

> "Give me back my grain of rice now, Granny."

She looked on the shelf.

The grain of rice was *gone*.

> "I am sorry, little sparrow, I believe your grain of rice has gotten lost."

That sparrow was indignant.

He began to hop up and down and squall.

> "GONE?
>
> GONE?
>
> That was my *special* grain of rice.
>
> That was my SPARROW'S LUCK!"

Granny tried to calm him down.

> "Never mind.
>
> Here, I will give you another grain of rice."

She opened her rice jar and took out a rice grain for him.

But sparrow would not accept it.

> "That is an *ordinary* grain of rice.
>
> Mine was a *lucky* grain of rice.
>
> My grain of rice was worth a whole HANDFUL of *your* rice."

Granny laughed.

> "All right little sparrow.
>
> Here is a whole handful of rice just for you."

And she put down a handful of rice for that sparrow.

Sparrow was delighted.
He began to hop up and down and sing . . .
    "Sparrow's LUCK!
    Sparrow's LUCK!"
And grain by grain, he carried it all back to his little nest and stored
    it away.

Then the sparrow began to think.
That rice made him think of something good to eat.
That rice made him think about payasam rice pudding.
Payasam was made from rice, and brown sugar, and milk . . . and it
    tasted SO good . . . it was just like CANDY!
        "I already have some *rice*," thought sparrow.
        "All I need to make payasam is some brown sugar and
            some milk!
        And a pot to cook it in.
        And some wood for my fire.
        Hmmmmm. . . ."

Then sparrow had an idea.
He flew right to the road where the street vendors passed.
Sparrow perched in a tree and waited.
After a while he saw a woodcutter coming down the road.
        "Here comes the wood for my fire!"
Sparrow began to hop up and down in the tree calling
        "Bad NEWS!
        Bad NEWS!
        Bad NEWS for the WOODCUTTER!"
The Woodcutter stopped and looked up at the little sparrow in the
    tree.

"What news for me, little sparrow?"
"You'd better go home AT ONCE!" said the sparrow.
You're . . . grandmother just died!"

"My GRANDMOTHER?
Oh, NO!"
The woodcutter dropped his bundle of wood and ran back up the
road.

Little Sparrow began to hop up and down and laugh.
"Sparrow's LUCK!
Sparrow's LUCK!"
He came down from the tree and gathered a nice little bundle of
wood for himself.
Then he carried that home and stuffed it into his nest.

"Now I have rice for my payasam and wood to cook it.
What else will I need?. . . .
Brown sugar.
Hmmmm. . . ."

Little Sparrow flew back to his tree by the road.
He waited and waited . . .
who did he see coming down the road . . .
a brown sugar seller!
"Bad NEWS!
Bad NEWS!
Bad NEWS for the BROWN SUGAR SELLER!" called
sparrow.
The brown sugar seller stopped and looked up into the tree.
"What are you saying, little sparrow?"

"You had better go home AT ONCE!"

165

"Why is that?"

"Your. . . . .HOUSE IS ON FIRE!"

"My HOUSE is on fire!
Oh, NO!"
And the brown sugar seller dropped his sugar and ran for home.

Sparrow jumped in his tree and chortled.
"Sparrow's LUCK!
Sparrow's LUCK!"
Down he came and gathered together enough brown sugar for his
payasam.
Then he carried it home and put it into his nest.
"Now I have rice and brown sugar and wood to cook my
payasam.
I still need . . . milk.
Hmmmmmm. . . ."

Back he flew to his roadside tree.
He waited and waited . . .
who did he see coming down the road . . .
the milk seller!
"Bad NEWS!
Bad NEWS!
Bad NEWS for the MILK SELLER!"
The milk seller stopped and looked up into the tree.
"What news is that, little sparrow?"

"You had better go home AT ONCE!"

"But why?"

"Your. . . .cow just fell down the well!

"My COW!
Oh, NO."
The milk seller dropped his milk containers and ran back up the road.

Sparrow began to hop up and down.
  "Sparrow's LUCK!
  Sparrow's LUCK!"
Sparrow carried his milk home to his nest.
  Now I have rice and brown sugar and milk and wood for
    my fire . . .
  But I still need one thing . . .
  a pot to cook it in.
  Hmmmmm. . . ."

Sparrow flew back to his tree by the road.
He waited and waited.
He waited and waited.
At last who should come down the road but . . .
  a pot seller!
This man was carrying shiny brass vessels, just right for cooking.
  "Bad NEWS!
  Bad NEWS!
  Bad NEWS for the POT SELLER!"
The pot seller stopped and peered up into the tree.
  "What are you saying, little sparrow?"

  "You had better go home AT ONCE!"

  "Why is that?"

  "Your . . . baby got his head stuck in a pot!"

"My BABY!
Oh, NO!"
The pot seller dropped his pots in the road and ran for home.

Sparrow began to hop up and down.
"Sparrow's LUCK!
Sparrow's LUCK!"
Sparrow looked through all of those pots and picked one just the right
size to cook his payasam.
Then he hurried back to his nest.
"Now I have *everything!*
Now I can make PAYASAM!"

Sparrow arranged his wood.
He lit his fire.
He put on his pot and poured brown sugar into it.
He put in the milk.
He put in the rice.
Everything melted together and began to cook.
It smelled SO good.
Sparrow could hardly wait to taste it.
At last it was done.
But it was so hot.
Still, Sparrow just couldn't wait any longer.
He stuck his wingtip in and flicked a bite into his beak.
"OW!"
It was SO hot that it burned his little wingtip and *scalded* his little
tongue!
"TOO HOT!"

That angry sparrow grabbed up the pot of payasam and *threw* it into
the well.

The pot sank into the water.
     "Oh oh.
     Maybe I shouldn't have done that."

Well at least the payasam would cool in the well.
Sparrow waited a few minutes.
Then he tried to fish out his pot of payasam.
But by this time all of the payasam had dissolved into the well water.
There was only a small bit left on the pot's brim.
Sparrow tasted that.
It was SO good.
Imagine what a whole potful would have been like.

Then Sparrow thought,
     "The payasam dissolved into the water.
     Maybe it is still in the well."
He tasted the water.
     "Mmmmm. . . ."
It was sweet like brown sugar.
It was creamy like milk and rice.
That water tasted just like payasam!
     "I can still have my payasam!"

That sparrow began to drink the well water.
He drank and he drank.
It tasted so good that he could not stop.
Sparrow drank . . . he drank . . . he drank . . .
He drank up the entire WELL full of water.

It made him SO fat . . . he could hardly wobble.
He was so stuffed that the well water started to spill back out of his
    beak.

Sparrow did not want to loose one drop of that wonderful payasam so he stuffed his beak shut with grass to keep the water from spilling out.

That greedy bird was so fat that he couldn't even climb back into his nest,

so he stumbled to granny's house and asked if he could sleep there for the night.

"Well you foolish little sparrow.
You have eaten too much for sure," said Granny.
"But go ahead and sleep in my cow shed if you like."

So little sparrow crawled into the cow shed and fell asleep.

During the night the cow woke up and looked over at the sleeping sparrow with the grass stuffed into its beak.

"Hmm . . . good grass . . ." thought the cow.

And reaching down, she pulled the grass from the sparrow's beak to munch it.

Bad news.

As soon as that grass was pulled from the sparrow's beak the well water in his stomach began to rush out.

It came out with such force that it washed that cow right out of the stable.

It washed that stable right out of the yard.

It washed granny right out of her house.

"Whew" said the empty little sparrow.
"That feels better."

And he flew back to his nest, calling down to the floating cow and the floating granny:

"Sparrow's LUCK!

Sparrow's LUCK!
Sparrow's LUCK!"

And that's the story of the little sparrow who made payasam.

NOTES ON TELLING

It works well to let the audience provide some of the information for this story line. Once you have established what items sparrow needs for his payasam you can let your audience tell you who he sees coming down the road. "Sparrow waited and waited . . . and who did he see coming down the road . . . ?" Whichever vendor they suggest is fine. You have to tell about each vendor and the order in which they arrive can be flexible.

I usually suggest a disaster at home for the first two vendors, then let the audience give little sparrow his idea for the last three. Sparrow pauses, trying to think up a good excuse to send the vendor home. "Your. . . ." Let the audience suggest what he told them and use one of their suggestions as sparrow's reply.

And of course most audiences will want to chant with you on the chirp-like "Sparrow's LUCK! Sparrow's LUCK!" refrains.

Since the crazy ending is unusual for our audiences, I sometimes warn the audience when I reach the line "Bad news." "Now the story gets REALLY silly. Are you ready? Here we go!" The wild flooding sequence of events is then delivered in a rapidly paced ending.

COMPARATIVE NOTES

This is expanded from "The Sparrow and the Sweet Pudding" in *Folktales of India*, edited by Brenda E.F. Beck, Peter J. Claus, Praphulladatta Goswami, and Jawahralal Handoo. The tale was collected by Dr. V. Saraswati Venugopal of the Tamil Department, University of Madurai. Dr. Vanugopal heard the tale as a child from her Ayyar Brahman mother, while growing up in Sattur village near Virudunagar in Ramnad District, Tamilnadu around 1945. She heard it again thirty years later from a friend in a Brahman home in Madurai.

Radhika Kumar of Seattle heard this story many times from her paternal grandmother, who grew up in the Palghat District of Kerala. She points out that this is a sanitized version of the story. Traditionally, the sparrow stuffs the straw in another orifice to hold the water. When it is pulled out, he is washed away. I have made a slight adjustment in the tale's ending to make it usable in our classrooms.

The story is told to caution children against impatience. It can also be used to put children to sleep, as sparrow goes for one rice grain at a time until the child nods off. Mrs. Kumar notes that this story is from South India and suggests that it be used with the Deepavali customs of South India.

The tale begins with a ploy similar to Motif K251.1 *The eaten grain and the cock as damages* as sparrow claims damages for his lost grain of rice. Thereafter the tale switches to a different motif K341 *Owner's interest distracted while goods are stolen.* No tale quite like this one is cited in Stith Thompson's *Motif-Index of Folk-Literature,* however.

DEEPAVALI/DIWALI

An Indian tradition.

Diwali takes place at the dark of the moon, usually eighteen days after Dasera. In the north of India, the holiday falls during the month of Kartiki, sometime in October or November. In South India, the holiday, Deepavali, is celebrated earlier, during the months named Aipashi or Thula (also October-November). Deepavali means: Deep = light + avali = string of—a string of lights. It is a spectacular holiday, with strings of pottery oil lamps lit to guide ancestral spirits on their visits to relatives and their return to heaven.

Since India is a large country with many distinct cultures, the customs surrounding this holiday vary from region to region. In all areas, this is a time of renewal, however. Homes are cleaned and flower garlands, often bright yellow and orange marigolds, may decorate doorways. Women decorate their doorsteps with intricate designs called *alpana,* in Northern India and *kolam* in South India. These are made by dribbling a flour paste onto the floor in a pattern. In some areas the *kolam/alpana* are colored, in others they are white.

In many areas Lakshmi, the Goddess of Wealth, is associated with this festival. On Diwali night Lakshmi visits every house. She must find the homes sparkling clean and the family all freshly bathed, in clean outfits, or she will refuse to let them prosper in the coming year. In Bengal, the goddess Kali is honored. Many small shrines to the blue-skinned goddess are created for this festival and the holiday climaxes as the Kali figures are carried in procession to the river and set afloat. The Jains use this festival time to honor Jaina deities. In some areas the coronation of Prince Rama is celebrated at this time. Though various deities may be associated with the celebration, the festival always incorporates a galaxy of shining clay oil lamps, fireworks, and general feasting and celebration. Huge bonfires may be lit as well.

SUGGESTIONS FOR A DEEPAVALI/DIWALI CELEBRATION

Decorate your space with garlands of marigolds, yellow chrysanthemums, or yellow crepe paper flowers.

Make small clay bowl lamps. Fill them with oil. Add a wick and watch them burn. These are simply made by rolling a ball of clay, flattening the top, pulling out one end into a trough for a spout, and hollowing out a recess in the top to hold the oil. A bit of oil is poured into the bowl and a string wick left with one end in the bowl of oil and one end hanging out of the spout.

Make *kolam* designs. Look at pictures of *kolam* or *alpana* designs in books and then design your own. Simple designs can be formed by drawing a series of dots in straight lines. Use these as a guide as you sprinkle colored flour or colored sand around them (see diagram). Small children can make interesting designs working in concentric circles or concentric squares. Coat a paper with liquid starch and dribble colored sands or colored flour onto the paper to make a design. Or draw designs with colored chalk on a sidewalk near your library or school. Our group drew designs on the cement pathways in our library courtyard and let them remain until the rain washed them away. One design is shown in *The Festival* by Peter Bonnici. For more designs see *Traditional Designs from India for Artist and Craftsmen* by Produmna Tana. To make multiple designs, fashion a template from a shoe box lid, a piece of heavy-duty craft foil, or a foil pan. Poke holes to create your designs. Fill the template with flour or sand and pat it down gently onto the surface where you wish to leave the *kolam* pattern. A large area can be covered

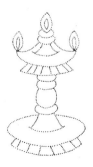

with *kolam* using this technique. Traditionally, the design may cover the entrance to a home or the floor of the prayer room. The design shown here is one used on a traditional silver or brass lamp, which is lit in every prayer room during Deepavali in South India. Enlarge this design to fit your box lid.

Serve sweet rice pudding treats.

FOR MORE INFORMATION ABOUT DIWALI

"Diwali" in *Festivals for You to Celebrate* by Susan Purdy (Philadelphia: J.B. Lippincott, 1969), pp. 41–42. Directions for making an *alpana*.

"Diwali" in *The Folklore of World Holidays* by Margaret Read MacDonald (Detroit: Gale Research, 1992), pp. 530–532.

"Diwali or Deepavali: The Festival of Lights" in *India Celebrates* by Jane Werner Watson, ilus. by Susan Andersen (Champaign, Ill.: Garrard, 1974), pp. 59–66.

Traditional Designs from India for Artists and Craftsmen by Produmna Tana (New York: Dover, 1981).

BOOKS TO SHARE

"Diwali—Festival of Lights" and "Lakshmi and the Clever Washerwoman" in *Seasons of Spendour: Tales, Myths and Legends of India* by Madhur Jaffrey (New York: Atheneum, 1985), p. 80; pp. 81–84. This collection includes stories for eleven Indian holidays.

The Festival by Peter Bonnici. Illus. by Lisa Kopper (Minneapolis: Carolrhoda, 1983). A young boy's first chance to dance with the men at his village festival. Shows his mother making *alpana*.

First Rains by Peter Bonnici. Illus. by Lisa Kopper (Minneapolis: Carolrhoda, 1984). A young boy waits for the first rains of the monsoon season to arrive.

Jyoti's Journey by Helen Ganly (London: Andre Deutsch, 1986). Jyoti attends her cousin's festive wedding then leaves on a plane for England. Unusual wallpaper-cut illustrations.

Savitri: A Tale of Ancient India by Aaron Shepard. Illus. by Vera Rosenberry (Morton Grove, Ill.: Albert Whitman & Co., 1992). Picture-book rendition of epic from the *Mahabharata*.

YAO JOUR

A Hmong folktale.

Yao Jour was an orphan.
His parents had died when he was very young.
So Yao Jour had to raise himself.
But he grew into a fine young man.
And his heart was good.

Because he was without family,
Yao Jour had no rice fields to farm.
He had to gather food from the forest for his needs.

One day when Yao Jour was in the forest hunting for birds,

175

he noticed a huge mushroom growing on the forest floor.

It was the largest mushroom he had ever seen.

"This mushroom deserves room to *grow*," said Yao Jour.

And he stopped his hunting and took time to clear away the weeds
    from around the mushroom, so it would have space.

As he turned to go, he heard a strange sound.

Turning he saw the mushroom beginning to *grow*!

It swelled and swelled.

Then suddenly POOF!

The mushroom disappeared.

And in it's place stood a little old woman.

She was as grey as the mushroom had been!

"*You* are Yao Jour," she said.

"I've seen you hunting in these forests before.

You have a kind heart.

You took the time to clear out all of these weeds so I could
    grow.

Now, I will repay you for that kindness.

You are an orphan.

I know all about you, Yao Jour.

No one cooks for you.

You live alone.

I will be your granny.

Come here each evening . . .

and I will have your supper ready for you.

Now run along.

But remember to come back."

176

That evening Yao Jour went to the clearing in the forest.
There was a meal waiting for him . . .
cooked by the little old woman.
Every night after that Yao Jour went into the forest.
And every night the old woman prepared a fine meal.

One evening after he had eaten, the old woman asked,
  "Isn't tomorrow the beginning of the New Year Festival?"
  "I think it is, " said Yao Jour.
  "But I have never gone to the festival."

  "You need to go to the *festival*," said the old woman.
  "All the girls will be there.
  They will be dressed in their prettiest clothes.
  They will be looking at all the boys.
  It's time for you to meet a young girl."

  "I have nothing to wear but these ragged old clothes you
   see me wearing.
  I could not go to a festival dressed like this."

  "Is there a big rock behind your house?"

  "Yes, a *very* big rock."

  "Go home and look behind that rock."

Yao Jour went home.
He looked behind the big rock.
There was a bamboo case.
He picked it up and shook it.
Out fell beautiful clothing!

Out fell a neck ring and bracelets!
When Yao Jour put these things on, he looked SO handsome.

Next day, Yao Jour bathed.
He washed his hair and fixed it just so.
He put on his fine clothing and his ornaments.
Then Yao Jour went to the New Year Festival.

When the girls saw him coming they asked
       "Who is that handsome young man?"
No one recognized him in his fine clothing.
       "Who could that *be?*"

The daughter of the headman to the north ran up and grabbed his
    right hand.
The daughter of the headman to the south ran up and grabbed his left
    hand.
They didn't let go.
They danced together . . . holding hands like that.
They sat and talked . . . holding hands.
They danced some more.
Those girls would not let him go.

When night came, Yao Jour *pulled* his hands free and ran from the
    festival.
Those two girls went looking for him.
       "Have you seen a handsome young man pass by here?"
       "Did you notice a young man in fine clothing go this way?"
No one had seen him.
They came to Yao Jour's house.
He had put his old clothing back on.
He had smeared ashes on his face.

He was sitting by the fire with his head bent.

"Have you seen a handsome young man?"

He shook his head.

"No."

The girls went on.

The daughter of the headman to the north went right on.

But the daughter of the headman to the south came back and looked closely at Yao Jour.

Then she went away.

Next day Yao Jour went to the festival again.

Those two girls grabbed his hands.

They danced with him, both holding his hands.

They talked with him.

They danced some more.

They wouldn't let him go.

When evening came Yao Jour *pulled* his hands free and ran away from the festival.

The girls searched everywhere for him.

"Have *you* seen a handsome young man?"

"Did a beautiful young person go past here?"

They came to Yao Jour's house.

He had put on his old clothing.

He had rubbed mud onto his face.

He sat by the fire with his head down.

"Did you see a handsome young man pass this way?"

"No."

The girls went on.

The daughter of the headman to the north went right on.

But the daughter of the headman to the south came back and looked at him closely.

Then she went away.

The next day when Yao Jour reached the festival only the daughter of
    the headman to the north was there.
She held *both* of his hands.
They danced all day.
They talked.
And they danced some more.

But Yao Jour was not happy.
He had *liked* that daughter of the headman to the south.
He wanted to see her smile again.

In the evening Yao Jour pulled his hands free and ran from the
    festival.

When he reached his house . . .
There sat the daughter of the headman to the south.
Waiting . . . by his door.

      "How did you *know?*"

      "When you *love* someone," she said.
      "Even if they cover their face with ashes . . .
      even if they cover their face with mud . . .
      if you *love* someome . . .
      you will *know* them."

So Yao Jour and the daughter of the headman to the south were
    married.
            "But you need land to support this new wife," said the
                mushroom woman.

"Go to that big rock behind your house.
Build a fire there.
Watch the fire for three days.
See what happens."

Yao Jour built a fire on that huge rock.
He watched that fire.
He kept the fire hot.
On the third day the rock SPLIT open.
And from the rock rushed out three streams of water!
Those streams cut a path through the forest.
And where they flowed, three rice paddies formed.

Yao Jour farmed those rice paddies all of his days . . .
and he lived there with his wife . . .
and their many many children.

NOTES ON TELLING

This tale seems popular with middle-grade listeners. The notion of the girls holding onto Yao Jour as they dance seems to intrigue them. I mime this slightly, as if my hands were held tight in the grasp of those two girls until I pull them free. The story is told in a straightforward manner, without audience participation.

COMPARATIVE NOTES

This tale is retold from a version in *The Religion of the Hmong Njua* by Nusit Chindarsi (Bangkok: Siam Society, 1976), pp. 179–180. This is a male Cinderella theme (R221). Orphan Yao Jour is provided clothing by a "fairy godmother," goes to the dance and meets his true love. This variant only mentioned two visits to the dance, however it seems likely that he would have gone on every day of the New Year Festival. I elaborated the tale to three visits in my telling. There is only one disappointed girl in this tale. His true love recognizes him and comes to his home despite his attempts to disguise himself in ashes. The three streams from a stone at the story's end seem a distincly Hmong addition to the tale. One wonders if this refers to an historical happening, since building a fire on top of a rock *could* cause it to split open. I have omitted a description of the old woman's fate from my tale, but the original tells us: "The old woman told him that she was very old and she was going to die. She asked Yao Jour to dig a grave to bury her, and told him that if he heard anything fall into the grave, he should fill it up, because it would mean she had died in it."

In the same collection is found a Cinderella story, "Gonao," in which a poor girl is given clothes by her mother in the form of a beheaded cow. It contains the lost slipper motif and an extended ending in which Gonao marries, has children, and is tracked down by the jealous stepsister.

If you wish to compare this with variants of the Cinderella tale see the citations in Margaret Read MacDonald's *The Storyteller's Sourcebook* under R221 *Three-fold flight from ball*. Use also Judy Sierra's *The Oryx Multicultural Series: Cinderella* for a collection of Cinderella tales along with suggested classroom activities.

HMONG NEW YEAR FESTIVAL
A tradition of the Hmong people.

The Hmong New Year traditionally begins at cockcrow on the first day of the waxing moon of the twelfth month. However, the actual date of the New Year celebration varies, being set to occur after the harvest is over. Each village plans its own festival, arranged so that the young people might be able to attend those in neighboring vilages as well.

The Hmong New Year Festival lasts three days and is a time for feasting, visiting, and showing off one's finest clothing and jewelry. This is traditionally a time of courtship. A special game is played in which couples toss a soft cloth ball back and forth. The one who drops the ball must give a forfeit to the other person, or sing a song.

The New Year Festival has included a fight between bulls too, but the fight is stopped if either animal is in danger of becoming seriously injured.

SUGGESTIONS FOR A HMONG NEW YEAR CELEBRATION

Make cloth balls. Use brightly colored cotton. Older children can cut balls from a pattern and sew them together. Younger children simply put stuffing in the middle of a cloth square, pull up the ends, and tie them shut with yarn.

Play the Hmong ball-tossing game. Stand in two lines and toss the cloth ball back and forth. Whenever a person drops the ball that person must sing a short song.

Share more Hmong folktales. Try *Folk Stories of the Hmong* by Norma Livo and Dia Cha or *Stories in Thread* by Marsha MacDowell. "The Tiger Steals Nkauj Ncoom" in *Folk Stories of the Hmong* (p. 101–105) tells of a girl raised by a tiger who returns to play ball at the New Year festival.

TO LEARN MORE ABOUT THE HMONG NEW YEAR

Folk Stories of the Hmong: Peoples of Laos, Thailand and Vietnam by Norma J. Livo & Dia Cha (Englewood, CO.: Libraries Unlimited, Inc., 1991). Information about Hmong culture and a collection of Hmong folktales. See p. 8 for information about the New Year celebration.

"Hmong New Year" in *Folklore of World Holidays* by Margaret Read MacDonald (Detroit: Gale Research, 1991), p. 44.

Stories in Thread: Hmong Pictorial Embroidery Project. Coordinated by Marsha Mac-Dowell. Michigan Traditional Arts Program. Folk Arts Division (East Lansing: Michigan State University Museum, 1989). Color plates of Hmong story cloths with commentary and a tape of one story "The Tiger and the Hunter" told by Pa Chai Vang.

THE SILVER PINE CONES

A folktale from Germany.

In the Black Forest of Germany there once lived a mother and father
    and seven children.
It was hard to find food enough for seven children.
The family was poor, but they survived.

Then one year, just before Christmas, the father fell ill.
He could not go into the forest to hunt.
So the family had no meat.
He could not go into the forest to cut wood.
Soon the family had no wood left for a fire.

On Christmas Eve the children sat cold and hungry.

The father lay in bed, quite sick.

"I will go into the forest and gather pinecones," said the
mother.

"Then at least we will have a warm fire.

And the sweet scent of burning pine may cheer us."

The woman took her basket and entered the dark forest.

But she could find no pine cones.

Deeper and deeper into the forest she wandered.

Suddenly she came into a glade surrounded by tall pines.

Overjoyed, she began to gather up handfuls of pinecones from the
forest floor.

But as soon as the first pinecone hit the bottom of her basket . . .

a fierce voice spoke out!

"BY MY BOOTS AND BY MY BEARD!
WHO'S STEALING MY PINECONES?"

"It's just me," gasped the frightened woman.

There behind her stood a dwarf.

He was short but very stout.

On his feet he wore big black boots.

On his face he wore a long grey beard and a terrible scowl.

"BY MY BOOTS AND BY MY BEARD!
WHY ARE YOU STEALING MY PINE CONES?"

"My husband is sick and cannot cut wood.

My children are cold and hungry.

I was gathering pinecones to make a fire this Christmas
　　Eve.
I didn't know they were *yours*."

"BY MY BOOTS AND BY MY BEARD!
PUT THOSE PINE CONES BACK!"

The woman put the pine cones back where she had found them.
She picked up her basket and started to leave.
The dwarf stroked his beard and scowled.

BY MY BOOTS AND BY MY BEARD!
YOU'LL FIND MORE DOWN THAT PATH!"

"Oh, THANK YOU!" The woman hurried down the path in
　　the direction he had pointed.

Sure enough. There was another grove of pines.

The woman stopped to gather a handful of the pine cones.
She tossed them into her basket.
But as soon as the first pine cone hit the bottom of the basket,
pine cones began to pelt down from the trees!
From all around they rained down.
Pine cones fell on the woman's head.
Pine cones fell into her basket.
Pine cones fell until they covered the ground.
And still they did not stop.

"Bewitched! Bewitched!
This place is bewitched!
The woman grabbed her basket and ran from the magic pine grove.

Behind her she heard a fierce voice booming out:
"BY MY BOOTS AND BY MY BEARD!
THAT OUGHT TO BE ENOUGH PINE CONES!"
The woman ran for home as if a forest full of dwarves were after her.
As she got closer to home, her basket seemed to become heavier and
heavier.
By the time she had reached her little cabin she could barely carry it.
She pushed open the cabin door and fell inside.
Her basket dropped to the floor and turned over.
Pine cones rolled across the floor.

The children sat up crying, "Oh MAMA!"
For the pine cones which were rolling across the floor were not
ordinary pine cones . . .
They were cones of solid silver!

"It's enchantment! Wicked enchantment!" cried the mother.

"Wait a moment," said the father.
"Tell me what happened in the forest."

So the mother told about the dwarf and the forest which had pelted
her with pine cones.

"This is not *bad* magic," said the father.
"This is *good* magic.
That dwarf you met in the forest must have been King
Laurin, the Dwarf King himself!
He is known to be very grumpy.
But he is also known to have a kind heart where poor
people are concerned.
He has tried to help us!

187

You must take some of these silver pine cones to town and
  sell them.
You will be able to buy food and wood!
Our fortune has changed!"

So the mother went to town with three silver pine cones.
And when she had sold them there was enough money to buy food
  for the family and gifts for the children besides!

What a feast they had that Christmas Day!
But the father still lay ill in his bed.

After Christmas dinner was done, the mother took raisins and spices
  and made a Christmas cake.
She iced it prettily, wrapped it, and placed it in her basket.
Then she set off for the forest once more.

When she reached the pine forest of the Dwarf King Laurin, the
  mother set the cake gently on the ground and started to leave.

A fierce voice boomed after her.
        "BY MY BOOTS AND BY MY BEARD!
        WHAT'S THE MEANING OF THIS?"

        "It's a gift.
        I wanted to thank you."

The Dwarf King grumbled and stroked his beard.
        "BY MY BOOTS AND BY MY BEARD.
        THEN I'LL GIVE *YOU* A GIFT!"

The Dwarf King leaned over and scraped away the snow from the
  ground.

He picked a small herb that was growing there beneath the snow and
handed it to the woman.
"BY MY BOOTS AND BY MY BEARD!
MAKE TEA FOR YOUR SICK HUSBAND!"

The woman took the herb and hurried from the forest.
She put the herb in a pot of water.
She boiled it and made tea.
But when the tea was done the water was a bright GREEN!

"Husband this is bad magic.
Maybe the Dwarf King sent you poison."

"Would the Dwarf King send us silver yesterday and poison
us today?" said her husband.
"Give it to me. I will drink it."
And the husband drank down all of that green tea.

As soon as he had swallowed the tea, his health returned.
The strength came back to his arms.
His head cleared.
He was as well as ever.

From that day on things went well for this family.
The children grew and prospered.
They worked hard and earned their daily bread.
But once in a while, when something special was needed, the mother
would go to town and sell a silver pine cone.
Much joy came of them.

But all of the pine cones were not sold.
One silver pine cone was given to each child for a keepsake.

Those children are grown now
and their children are grown.
But I am told that each family still treasures its silver pine cone . . .
a remembrance of the gift of Dwarf King Laurin.

NOTES ON TELLING

The Dwarf King's voice should boom loudly. I pound my fists into my palms. First right into left, then left into right, as I chant his "By my boots and by my beard!"

You may want to have a basket of pine cones on hand to display before you tell the story.

COMPARATIVE NOTES

A brief version of this story is given in *Myths and Legends of Flowers, Trees, Fruits, and Plants in All Ages and In All Climes* by Charles M. Skinner (Philadelphia: J. B. Lippincott, 1911, 1925), pp. 114–225. The story is said to take place in the Hartz Mountains on a hill known as the Hubinchenstein. According to this account, people in this area gather pine cones at Christmas, silver them, and use them as ornaments. They say that the custom originated with this tale. A more elaborate version of the story is "Fir Cones" in *A Book of Dwarfs* by Ruth Manning-Sanders (New York: Dutton, 1963), pp. 125–128. She adds the sick-husband motif. Manning-Sanders calls the Dwarf King "Gubich, King of the Dwarfs". I have named my Dwarf King after the Dwarf King Laurin of Ruth Sawyer's Austrian tale, "Schnitzle, Schnotzle, and Schnootzle" in *The Long Christmas*, in order to be able to connect the two stories when I tell them both.

This is Motif F451.5.1.4 *Dwarf's gold. Seemingly worthless gift given by dwarf turns to gold* and F451.5.1.10 *Dwarfs heal (give medicine).*

CHRISTMAS IN GERMANY

The Christmas season begins with the first Sunday of Advent, four weeks before the Sunday preceeding Christmas. An Advent wreath is hung up, with four candles, one to be lit each Sunday until Christmas Sunday. On December 1, children begin opening the little windows on their Advent calendars. These are elaborate pictures with a tiny cardboard window to pull open for each day until Christmas.

On December 4, Saint Barbara's Day, cherry branches are cut and put in water by the stove so they will blossom by Christmas. December 6 is Saint Nicholas' Day. Saint Nicholas arrives wearing a bishop's robe with Bishop's mitre and staff. He questions the children about their behavior during the year and distributes presents from the sack his attendants carry. He is accompanied by a black figure who is known by various names in different parts of Germany but is most commonly called Knecht Ruprecht. Knecht Ruprecht carries the sack of treats, but also has a rod and is meant to beat misbehaving children. German parents may threaten children who do not mind, "Just wait till Ruprecht comes!"

In some areas St. Nicholas does not come in person but slips his presents into the children's shoes, which are left out by the fireplace.

Saint Nicholas's Day is the time for the Christkindlmarkt to open in many cities. This is a street fair which runs until Christmas selling toys, decorations, and Christmas sweets.

Children in Germany write letters to the Christ Child asking for Christmas gifts. Or in Northern Germany they write to Father Christmas. The letter for the Christ Child is left on a window-sill with a little sugar sprinkled on it to attract the Christ Child's attention. Some children mail their letters to post offices of towns with names like "Himmelreich" (Kingdom of Heaven), "Himmelstadt" and "Himmelstur". Children paste silver stars on their windows to show the Christ Child the way to their homes.

The Christmas tree is traditionally lit with candles, and decorated with gilded nuts, red apples, and candies wrapped in tinsel paper, as well as glass ornaments, paper chains, and angel hair. Gingerbread figures and cookies are hung on last of all. On Christmas Eve the Christmas Tree is lit and a bell is rung to let the children know that the Christ Child or Father Christmas has arrived with the presents. They fling open the door and rush into the room to gasp in awe. The family then sings a hymn such as Stille Nacht and O Tannenbaum and only after that moment are the presents passed out. In Northern Germany the "Julklapp" tradition is celebrated. On Christmas Eve the door opens just a crack and nuts and packages are tossed in as if by magic. These packages contain parcels within parcels and each may be addressed to a different person . . . so the package is passed around and around the room as it is opened and opened again, until the actual prize is found deep inside the bundle.

The Christmas Eve supper features carp, goose or other special foods depending on the area. Afterward, the family attends Midnight Mass. Some families fast on Christmas Eve day and hold their feast after Midnight Mass.

On Christmas Day itself another feast occurs . . . the Grosses Weihnachtsfest, the Big Christmas Feast! Of course there are many sweet treats, cookies of every sort, chocolate pretzels, fruit cakes, and stollen. Dinner may be a roast hare or a stuffed goose. And always there are bowls of apples, nuts, and fruit. The apple stands for the Tree of Knowledge in Paradise. Nuts remind of the difficulties and mysteries of life, and fruits recall the bounty of Christmas.

SUGGESTIONS FOR A GERMAN CHRISTMAS CELEBRATION

Paint pine cones with silver and fasten ribbons to them so they can be hung as ornaments.

Make bird feeder gifts from pine cones by coating them with suet and bird seed. Fasten a bit of nylon fishing line to the cone so it may be hung from a tree out of doors.

Tell or read "Schnitzle, Schnotzle, and Schnootzle" from *The Long Christmas* by Ruth Sawyer (New York: Viking, 1941), pp. 69–82. The Dwarf King Laurin rewards three kind boys with gold and silver treats.

Sing a carol in German, such as "Stille Nacht" (Silent Night) or "O Tannenbaum" (O Christmas Tree). Many carol books include the words in both German and English.

Snack on nuts, apples and fruit or on German Christmas pastries, such as gingerbread men.

FOR MORE INFORMATION ON CHRISTMAS IN GERMANY

Christmas in Germany (Lincolnwood, Ill.: Passport Books, 1991). Colorful illustrations to share.

Christmas in Germany. Bielefelder Kinderchor (Hollywood, Ca.: Capital Records 4X33214, 1986). Casette. German Christmas music.

PAPA GOD AND THE PINTARDS

A folktale from Haiti.

Papa God planted a field of rice.
He was depending on that rice crop for the coming year.

One day Gabriel came in all in a huff.
  "Papa God! Papa God!
  The Pintard birds are down there eating up your rice field! "

Papa God jumped up.
  "Gabriel we can't have that.
  You take my shotgun and go down there and scare off those
    Pintards.
  Do it right away!"

Gabriel took Papa God's shotgun.
He ran down to that rice field.

But those Pintard birds saw him coming.
They flew up into a mimbron tree and began to sing and dance.

> "Here comes Gabriel!
> Here comes Gabriel!
> He's gotta big gun!
> He's gotta big gun!"

Those birds flapped their wings and *sang* and how they *danced*.

> "Here comes Gabriel!
> Here comes Gabriel!
> He's gotta big gun!
> He's gotta big gun!"

Gabriel heard that singing.
He saw that joyful dancing.
He just couldn't stop himself.
He began to sing and dance himself.

> "Here comes Gabriel!
> Here comes Gabiel!
> He's got a big gun!
> He's got a big gun!"

Gabriel danced with those Pintard birds all day long.
At dusk the birds flew away.
And Gabriel went home remembering what he had been told to do.
> "Papa God I didn't get around to scaring off those Pintard
> birds after all.

They were singing and dancing so pretty.
I just *couldn't* bear to shoot at them."
Papa God said "Well my goodness.
You've let me down Gabriel.
Tomorrow I'll send Peter down there and see what *he* can
    do."

So next day Peter took Papa God's shotgun and *he* went down to
    shoot those Pintards.
As soon as those birds saw him coming
they began to sing and dance.
    "Here comes Peter!
    Here comes Peter!
    He's got a big gun!
    He's got a big gun!"

Peter heard them.
He saw that *joyful* dancing.
He just couldn't help himself.
Peter began singing and dancing too.
    "Here comes Peter!
    Here comes Peter!
    With Papa God's gun!
    With Papa God's gun!"

He danced all that day.
At dusk those Pintard birds flew away.
They had sure eaten up a lot of that rice field.
Peter went back to Papa God.

    "Looks like I failed too, Papa God.

195

I'm sorry, but those Pintard birds can really sing and dance.
I just couldn't bear to shoot at them."

"Never mind," said Papa God.
"I'll go down tomorrow and do it myself."

Next morning Papa God took his big shot gun.
He went right down to that rice field.
Those Pintard birds saw him coming.
They began to dance around and sing DOUBLETIME.
"PapaGod! PapaGod! PapaGod! PapaGod!
Gotta big gun!
Gotta big gun!"

"PapaGod! PapaGod! PapaGod! PapaGod!
Gotta big gun!
Gotta big gun!"

Papa God heard that singing.
Papa God saw that joyful dancing.
He just couldn't help himself.
Papa God started in DANCING.
Papa God said,
"Let them HAVE my rice field.
These Pintard birds are just too wonderful to shoot!"

Then Papa God had an idea.
He rememberd those people he'd put down on earth.
They were always complaining about how miserable they were.
They never had enough to eat.
Things never quite suited them.
They were always so unhappy.

Papa God said,

> "I have a *wonderful* idea!
>
> I'll send these Pintard birds down to earth.
>
> They can sing and dance and just make those people feel
> HAPPY!"

So Papa God called Shango, the God of Thunder and Lightning.

Shango dropped a thunderbolt clear down to earth

and God slid those Pintard birds right down it.

Right down to Guinea in Africa.

That's where Papa God sent them.

And were they happy.

They arrived just singing.

> "Here come the Pintards
>
> Here come the Pintards
>
> We sing and we dance!
>
> We sing and we dance!"

And do you know to this day,

the people of Guinea sing and dance better than anyone in the world.

That's because they learned their singing and dancing directly from

> the Pintards that Papa God sent down.

NOTES ON TELLING

Invent your own tune for the Pintards song. If you aren't very musical you can simply chant the words and flap your wings a bit. Other tellers may want to sing AND dance with the Pintards.

Note that the story combines God, the angel Gabriel, and Saint Peter with Shango, the God of Thunder and Lightning.

A *pintard* is a guinea fowl. You might want to show Guinea on a map of the African continent after you tell this story. You might also want to show a photograph of guinea hens since many children will not recognize this farmyard bird.

COMPARATIVE NOTES

This story is retold from a tale that Zora Neal Hurston heard during her stay in Haiti, "Papa God and the Pintards." It is published in *Tell My Horse* by Zora Neal Hurston, pp. 259–261. A variant also appears in *The Piece of Fire and Other Haitian Tales* by Harold Courlander (New York: Harcourt, 1942, 1964), pp. 50–54. In this tale, the Vodoun priest advises tree lizard, Zandolite, to give a festival during the drought. God sends St. John to stop the noise. St. John is seated by the drummers and can't keep from dancing. St. Patrick, St. Peter, and God Himself follow. They dance, the drought ends.

This is a variant of Stith Thompson Motif K606.02 *Escape by teaching song to watchman*. Stith Thompson lists Kaffir, Cape Verde Islands, Gold Coast, Basuto, and Indonesian sources for this and similar tales. MacDonald's *Storyteller's Sourcebook* lists Eskimo, Russian, Cherokee, and Makah versions.

KWANZAA

An African-American tradition.

Kwanzaa is a seven day celebration begining on December 26 and ending on New Year's Day. This tradition was created in 1966 by Dr. Maulana (Ron) Karenga, a Californian who wanted to create a festival which could act as a focal point for black pride. He used elements from African harvest festivals and chose words from Swahili for his ceremonial objects. Swahili is a language used throughout East Africa to communicate between groups, since each tribal group has it's own distinct language or dialect.

The Kwanzaa celebration requires seven special objects. These are arranged as a centerpiece for the festive celebration:

- Mazao—fruits and vegetables, which stand for the product of unified effort.
- Mkeka—a straw mat, which represnts the reverence for tradition.
- Vibunzi—an ear of corn for each child in the family.
- Zawadi—simple gifts, these should be related to education and to African or African-influenced things.
- Kikombe cha umoja—a communal cup for the libation.
- Kinara—a seven-branched candleholder. This symbolizes the continent and peoples of Africa.
- Misumaa saba—seven candles, each symbolizes one of the seven principles of Kwanzaa, the Nguzo Saba.

On each day of Kwanzaa a family member lights one of the candles and discusses the principle represented on that day. The Swahili words for the seven principles of Kwanzaa are:

1. Umoja—Unity: To strive for and maintain unity in the family, community, nation, and race.
2. Kujichagulia—Self-Determination: To define ourselves, name ourselves, create for ourselves, and speak for ourselves instead of being defined, named, created for, and spoken for by others.
3. Ujima—Collective Work and Responsibility: To build and maintain our community together, and to make our sisters' and brothers' problems our problems and to solve them together.
4. Ujamaa—Cooperative Economics: To build and maintain our own stores, shops, and other businesses and to profit from them together.
5. Nia—Purpose: To make our collective vocation the building and developing of our community in order to restore our people to their traditional greatness.
6. Kuumba—Creativity: To do always as much as we can, in whatever way we can, in order to leave our community more beautiful and beneficial than we inherited it.
7. Imani—Faith: To believe with all our heart in our people, our parents, our teachers, our leaders, and in the righteousness and victory of our struggle.

December 31 or January 1 the Kwanzaa Karamu, a lavish feast featuring foods from African, Caribbean, and African-American traditions, is held. The following ceremony is suggested:

1. Kukaribisha—Welcoming: Introductory remarks and recognition of distinguished guests and elders.
   Cultural expression through song, music, dance, unity circles, etc.
2. Kukumbuka—Remembering: Reflections of a man, a woman, and a child.
   More cultural expression.
3. Kuchunguza tena na kutoa ahadi tena—Reassessment and Recommitment: Introduction of distinguished guest lecturer and short talk.
4. Kushangilia—Rejoicing:
   Tamshi la tambiko—libation statement.
   Kikombe cha umoja—unity cup.
   Kutoa majina—calling the names of ancestors and black heroes.
   Ngoma—drumming

Karamu—feast
More cultural expression.
5.   Tamshi la tutaonana—Farewell statement.

Each family or community is free to adapt these traditions to suit their own needs.

SUGGESTIONS FOR A KWANZAA CELEBRATION

Decorate your space with the Kwanzaa colors of green, red, and black.

Prepare a display with the seven objects of Kwanzaa.

Light the candles one at a time and discuss the seven principles of Kwanzaa. Seven individuals could be given the task of preparing brief comments, lighting candles.

Learn a song, dance, or singing game from an African culture.

Share African or African-American folktales.

Weave a placemat of red, green, and black strips or make a small clay candelabra with seven branches.

Share a feast of African, Caribbean, or African-American foods.

See also: West African Yam Festival, p. 159.

TO LEARN MORE ABOUT KWANZAA

"Introduction" to *Kwanzaa: An Africa-American Celebration of Culture and Cooking* by Eric V. Copage (New York: William Morrow, 1991), p. xiii-xxvi and "Nguzo Saba," pp. 1–12 and "Nguzo Saba," p. 321–330. Introduction with many suggestions for incorporating Kwanzaa into family life; 319 pages of recipes.

Kwanzaa: Everything You Always Wanted to Know but Didn't Know Where to Ask by Cedric McClester (New York: Gumbs & Thomas, 1985).

FOR ACTIVITIES SEE

"African and African-American Cultures" in *Cultural Awareness for Children* by Judy Allen, Earldene McNeill, and Velma Schmidt (New York: Addison-Wesley, 1992), pp. 3–33.

"African-American Materials and Programs" by Martha R. Ruff in *Venture into Cultures: A Resource Book of Multicultural Materials & Programs* by Carla D. Hayden, editor (Chicago: American Library Association, 1992), pp. 1–18.

BOOKS TO SHARE

Celebrating Kwanzaa by Diane Hoyt-Goldsmith. Photos by Lawrence Migdale. (New York: Holiday House, 1993). A Chicago family celebrates Kwanzaa.

Kwanzaa by Deborah Newton Chocolate (Chicago: Children's Press, 1990). A young boy's family celebrates Kwanzaa.

Seven Candles for Kwanzaa by Andrea Davis Pinkney. Illus. by Brian Pinkney (New York: Dial, 1993). Beautifully illustrated explanation of Kwanzaa.

GOING TO CERVIÈRES

A folktale from France.

The Storyteller Says:
    CRIC CRAC CLOG!
    WOODEN KITCHEN SPOON!
And the story can begin.

On Saint Sylvester's Day Grey Goose woke up with a *terrible*
    headache.
And no wonder.
Saint Sylvester's Day is December 31, or New Year's Eve.
Grey Goose always ate *so* many sweets during the holidays.
He had been stuffing himself on sweets ever since Christmas.

What do you think Grey Goose ate on Christmas Day?

Candy? That's right!

Cookies! He certainly did!

Cake? Oh yes! Cake too. Especially the kind with chocolate icing.

Grey Goose ate *all* those things on Christmas Day.

And there were so many sweet things left over *after* Christmas.

So Grey Goose ate cake and cookies and cupcakes and candies on
    December 26 too.

And he ate candy, and cookies and cake on December 27.

He ate candy and cookies and cake on December 28.

He ate candy and cookies and cake on December 29 . . .

and he ate. . . .candy and cookies and cake on December 30!

So by Saint Sylvester's Day . . . December 31 . . . it is no wonder
    that Grey Goose had a *terrible* headache.

"I am going on a *diet*." said Grey Goose.

"I am going to climb to Cervières for my health."

Now Cervières is high in the mountains.

The air is fresh there.

And the water is good.

And the walk up the mountain can't help but improve one's health.

So Grey Goose started the long climb to Cervières.

He was *so* fat

and *so ill*.

Grey Goose sang a little chant to help him on his way.

"Cric Crac Clog!

Wooden kitchen spoon!

If I walk today . . .
If I walk tomorrow . . .
If I walk
and I walk
I will go a long way!"
Chanting and marching, up the mountain he went.

After a while he met Black Cat.
"Bonjour Grey Goose," said Black Cat.
"Where are you going so early in the morning?"

"Bonjour Black Cat!
I have such a *terrible* headache.
I am going to Cervières for my health!"

"What a good idea!
May I come with you?
The fresh air would do me good."

"Eh bien," said Grey Goose.
"Come along."

So Black Cat and Grey Goose went up the mountain.

"Cric Crack Clog!
Wooden kitchen spoon!
If I walk today . . .
If I walk tomorrow . . .
If I walk
and I walk
I will go a long way!"

After a while they met Woolly Sheep.

"Bonjour Grey Goose.
Bonjour Black Cat.
Where are you going so early in the morning?"

"Bonjour Woolly Sheep," said Grey Goose.
It's like this . . .
I have a terrible headache.
We are going to Cervières for our health."

"What a good idea!
May I come with you?
The walk would do me good."

"Eh bien," said Grey Goose.
"Come along."

So Grey Goose, Black Cat, and Woolly Sheep went up the mountain.
Three friends. Traveling together.

"Cric Crac Clog!
Wooden kitchen spoon!
If I walk today . . .
If I walk tomorrow . . .
If I walk
and I walk
I will go a long way."

After a while they met Fat Cow.
Fat Cow was *so fat* because she had a baby in her tummy.
She was going to have a baby calf very soon.

"Bonjour Grey Goose.
Bonjour Black Cat.

205

Bonjour Woolly Sheep.
Where are you going so early in the morning?"

"Bonjour Fat Cow." said Grey Goose.
"It's like this . . .
I have a *terrible* headache.
We are going to Cervières for our health."

"What a good idea!" said Fat Cow.
"May I come with you?
The mountain air would be good for me and my baby too!"

"Eh bien," said Grey Goose.
"Come along."

So the four animals walked up the mountain to Cervières.
"Cric crac clog!
Wooden kitchen spoon!
If I walk today . . .
If I walk tomorrow . . .
If I walk . . .
and I walk . . .
I can go a long way."

They were swinging their arms and striding up that mountain.
Eh . . . eh . . . eh . . . eh . . .
Eh . . . eh . . . eh . . . eh. . . .

When night fell they were still walking.
But they were becoming tired.
Eh . . . eh . . .
Eh . . . eh. . . .

"Here is a little house.
I wonder if we could spend the night?"

The animals peeked in at the window.
What a poor little home it was.
There was one little chair.
There was one little table.
There was one little bed.
That was all.
In the fireplace three tiny pieces of wood were burning, hardly
enough to make any heat at all.
And on the chair sat an old woman.
She looked very sad.

She was talking to herself.
"How poor I am.
How poor I have become.
I don't even have a goose anymore to give me feathers for
my bed.
How poor I am.
How poor I have become.
I don't even have a cow anymore to give me a cup of milk
for my supper.
How poor I am.
How poor I have become.
I don't even have a woolly sheep anymore to give me wool
for a nice warm shawl.
How poor I am.
How poor I have become.
I don't even have a cat anymore to keep me company."

When the animals heard this they looked at one another.

That poor old woman.

She *needs us!*

"My headache is gone now," said Grey Goose.

"Let's stop and help this little old woman."

Grey Goose knocked on the door.

"Come in and welcome," called the old woman.

The animals went into the house.

"We were on our way to Cervières," said Grey Goose.

"But it is too dark to go on.

Might we spend the night with you?"

"Oh course," said the old woman.

"I am glad of the company!"

"We will be no trouble," said Black Cat.

"Grey Goose will make his bed in the hen house.

Woolly Sheep and Fat Cow will sleep in the stable.

And I, Black Cat, I will lie right here and keep an eye on
the fire."

So the four animals spent the night with the old woman.

And they felt so comfortable in her company that they decided to stay
right there and forget all about going to Cervières.

Why their health had improved just from the good company!

And perhaps the long walk had done them good as well.

So Grey Goose gave the old woman some soft feathers for her bed.

Fat Cow gave her a sweet little baby calf, and a cup of milk every
evening for her supper.

And Woolly Sheep gave her soft, warm wool to knit a shawl.

But best of all . . .

Black Cat stayed by the woman's side all day to keep her company.
And every night Black Cat sat in the old woman's lap and purred and
purred and purred.
> CRIC CRAC CLOG
> MY LITTLE TALE IS GONE.

NOTES ON TELLING

I teach the audience the storyteller's opening chant "Cric Crac Clog! Wooden
Kitchen Spoon!" before we begin the story, then let them chant it with me as we
start the tale.

It can be fun to play with the audience at the story's beginning, letting them
suggest just which goodies Grey Goose ate. "What do you think he ate that
Christmas Day?" "Candy canes? That's *right!* He remembered that candy canes
were hanging on the Christmas tree. So he ate them all!" "Chocolates?" "Yes! And
he ate a chocolate Santa Claus . . . and then he found a chocolate bunny left from
Easter. So he ate that too!" Let the audience members suggest sweet items, then
improvise your answers.

An alternative way to elaborate this story might be to make a list of French
confections and let Grey Goose pig out on ethnic treats.

After Grey Goose has completed his binge, it is clear why he has such a
headache. The audience will enjoy chiming in with you on certain phrases. When
Grey Goose exclaims "I am going to go on a . . . , let the audience add with you—
DIET." Each time Grey Goose relates his malady, let the audience join in on the
". . . .TERRIBLE HEADACHE."

When I first mention Cervières, I pause to let the audience breathe in that
fresh mountain air and sip that cold mountain water. Then once the animals are all
together and begin their final ascent I lead the group in an arm swinging, huffing
and puffing stride up the mountain. We rhythmically walk and walk, we breathe in
the fresh mountain air, we sip the fresh mountain water . . . all in rhythm. Then we
feel so much BETTER! THEN is gets dark.

End the story on a very soft purring. Then gently add the Cric Crac Clog
ending.

In telling this story, I have adapted an audience participation-improv technique used by Seattle storyteller Phyllis Silling. Phyllis oftens encourages her
audience to contribute suggestions for her story, then she improvizes on their ideas,
incorporating them into the story. The audience's range of possible suggestions is

fairly limited and your improvized incorporations need not be wildly imaginative to work. Try it and see if you enjoy this technique. For tellers with Phyllis's improvisational skill this can make for an exciting story event.

COMPARATIVE NOTES

This story is based on "The Four Friends" from *Folktales of France,* edited by Geneviève Massignon. Translated by Jacqueline Hyland (Chicago: University of Chicago Press, 1968). The tale was collected in Ponçins, in Forez, from an old miller's wife by Marguerite Gonon.

This is an unusual variant of Type 130 *The Animals in Night Quarters.* Usually the animals route robbers and take over a house. In many French variants the animals leave because their masters plan to butcher them for a New Year or Christmas feast. This gentle version is a delight to tell, with its unusual, kind ending. The *cric crac clog* chant is given as "the peasant storyteller's favorite introductory rhyme." I have altered it slightly to improve the rhythm and repeated it in the body of the story. I have not seen the original French. The English given by Hyland is "Cric-crac, clog, kitchen spoon—walk today, walk tomorrow, by walking and walking we cover a lot of ground."

The habit of going to rural spots and spas for one's health is still popular among Europeans.

SYLVESTER DAY

Sylvester Day was originally a day to honor Pope Sylvester, a Roman who was pope from 314–335. It was St. Sylvester who baptized Constantine the Great. Since this saint's day fell on New Years Eve, December 31, the day has acquired festive connotations. In Austria the year may be toasted in with "Sylvester Punch." In Switzerland the last person to awake on St. Sylvester's Day was taunted as a "Sylvester." Louise Patteson wrote of her Swiss childhood, "One year I was late in school on that day, and as I walked in, the roar of "Sylvester!" was so deafening that my knees caved. I had to catch hold of the door-latch to keep from falling." (From: *When I Was a Girl in Switzerland* by S. Louise Patteson. Boston: Lothrop, Lee & Shepard, 1921.)

A legend says that St. Sylvester captured a sea monster, the Leviathan. People believed that on New Year's Day in the year 1000 the imprisoned Leviathan would escape to destroy the earth. In the year 999 a new pope was chosen who was also named Sylvester. People were terrified. But on the first day of the year 1000 the Leviathan did not appear and the world did not come to an end, so people celebrated.

In 1582 Pope Gregory XII dropped ten days from the calendar and set up a new calendar which would keep the seasons in a constant place on the yearly calendar. Many European cultures still show vestiges of the pre-Gregorian calendar in their celebration of "Old Christmas" on January 6. Likewise, "Old Silvester" is still celebrated on January 13 as a New Year holiday in some areas. In Urnäsch, Switzerland, the *Silvesterchläusen* go from house to house singing and collecting drinks. They perform in elaborate costumes fashioned from greenery and carry huge bells.

SUGGESTIONS FOR A SYLVESTER DAY CELEBRATION

Act out the story "Going to Cervières."

Follow the story with a tasting contest for holiday sweets. Give each child a tiny portion and vote on the favorite sweet. Rate them on flavor, consistency, appearance, sweetness, etc.

Talk about dieting after eating too many sweets. Suggest diet foods. Suggest excercises to help lose weight.

Perform a set of excercises or go for a brisk walk for your health.

In Europe, people go to spas for their health. There they drink mineral waters and bathe in mineral pools. Have a mineral-water tasting contest.

Maria Augusta Trapp of the Trapp Family Singers gives a recipe for "Sylvester Punch" to be served on Sylvesterabend (The Eve of St. Sylvester). Her punch calls for warming a bottle of red wine with twelve cloves, the grated rind of a lemon, two tablespoons of sugar, and two cinnamon sticks. When this mixture is warm, but not boiling, add an equal amount of hot tea. A tasty hot drink for children could be concocted by substituting grape or apple juice for the wine. We grated the lemon rind, added the other ingredients, and put it on to simmer at the begining of our program. It was ready to drink by the end. (Recipe from *Around the Year with the Trapp Family* by Maria Augusta Trapp, New York: Pantheon, 1955, p. 69.)

If you wish to stress the *Sylvesterklausen* celebration of this holiday:

Look at pictures of the Swiss *Sylvesterklausen* celebration and create your own costumes from greenery. Then parade to show them off.

Or read *A Bell for Ursli* by Selina Chönz, then pass out bells and sing a few songs with bell accompaniment. Try the round "Christmas Bells" in *Booksharing: 101 Programs for Preschoolers* by Margaret Read MacDonald (Hamden, Conn.: Library Professional Publications, 1988), p. 246.

FOR MORE INFORMATION ABOUT SYLVESTER DAY

"Merrymaking in Austria" and "Sylvester Day and the Day After in Belgium" in *Happy New Year Round the World* by Lois S. Johnson (Chicago: Rand McNally, 1966), pp. 16–24.

"Sylvester Day" and "Old Silvester" in *Folklore of World Holidays* by Margaret Read MacDonald (Detroit: Gale Research, 1992), p. 29, p. 653.

"St. Sylvester's Eve" in *Holidays & Festivals: New Year* by Alan Blackwood (Vero Beach, Fl.: Rourke, 1987), pp. 40–41. Color photos and info on the Swiss Sylvesterklausen aspect of the celebration.

BOOKS TO SHARE

To stress a French cultural theme:

The Brave Little Goat of Monsieur Seguin: A Picture Story from Provence. Translated and adapted from a story by Alphonse Daudet. Illus. by Chiyoko Nakatani (Cleveland: World, 1968). A little goat's misadventures in the mountains near his home in the French countryside.

Spring-time for Jeanne-Marie by Françoise. (New York: Scribner's, 1955).
A lost duck on a little river in France.

To stress a Swiss/Austrian *Silvesterklausen* theme:

A Bell for Ursli by Selina Chönz. Illus. Alois Carigiet.
(New York: Walck, 1950).
Picture book of bell-carrying festival in the Austrian Alps.

BIBLIOGRAPHY OF WORKS CONSULTED
FOR TALES AND TALE NOTES

Aarne, Antti and Stith Thompson. *The Types of the Folktale: A Classification and Bibliography*. Folklore Fellows Communications, no. 184. Helsinki: Suomalainen Tiedeakatemia, 1973.

Achebe, Chinua. *Arrow of God*. New York: John Day, 1967, c. 1964.

Adams, Robert J. *Folktales of Japan*. Chicago: University of Chicago Press, 1963.

Barchers, Suzanne. *Wise Women: Folk and Fairy Tales from Around the World*. Englewood, Co.: Libraries Unlimited, 1990.

Beck, Brenda E. F., Peter J. Claus, Praphulladatta Goswami, and Jawahralal Handoo. *Folktales of India*. Chicago: University of Chicago, 1987.

Beckett, Hilary. *The Rooster's Horns*. New York: Collins and World, 1978.

Belpré, Pura. *Perez and Martina: A Portorican Folktale*. Illus. by Carlos Sanchez. New York: F. Warne, 1932.

Bonnet, Leslie. *Chinese Folk and Fairy Tales*. New York: Putnam, 1958.

Briggs, Katharine M. *A Dictionary of British Folk-Tales*. Part A, v. 1. Bloomington, Ind.: Indiana University Press, 1974.

Brown, Marcia. *Stone Soup*. New York: Scribners, 1979.

Bryan, Ashley. *The Cat's Purr*. New York: Atheneum, 1985.

Carter, Dorothy Sharp. *The Enchanted Orchard and Other Folktales of Central America*. New York: Harcourt, Brace, Jovanovich, 1973.

Chindarsi, Nusit. *The Religion of the Hmong Njua*. Bangkok: Siam Society, 1976.

Claudel, Calvin Andre. *Fools and Rascals: Louisiana Folktales* Baton Rouge, La.: Legacy Publishing, 1978.

Courlander, Harold. *The Piece of Fire, and Other Haitian Tales*. New York: Harcourt, Brace & World, 1964.

Credle, Ellis. *Tall Tales from the High Hills*. New York: Thomas Nelson, 1957.

Folk Tales from Asia for Children Everywhere. Book 2. New York: Weatherhill, 1975.

Folk Tales from China. Fourth Series. Peking: Foreign Language Press, 1958.

Glazer, Mark. *Flour From Another Sack & Other Proverbs, Folk Beliefs, Tales, Riddles & Recipes.* Edinburg, Tex.: Pan American University Press, 1982.

Green, Roger Lancelyn. *A Cavalcade of Dragons.* New York: Walck, 1971.

Greene, Ellin. *Clever Cooks: A Concoction of Stories, Charms, Recipes and Riddles.* Illus. by Trina Schart Hyman. New York: Lothrop, Lee & Shepard, 1973.

Hurston, Zora Neal. *Tell My Horse: Voodoo and Life in Haiti and Jamaica.* New York: Perennial Library, 1990. Reprint of 1938 ed.

Kawai, Hayao. *The Japanese Psyche: Major Motifs in the Fairy Tales of Japan.* Trans. by Hayao Kawai and Sachiko Reece. Dallas, Tex.: Spring Publications, Inc., 1988.

MacDonald, Margaret Read. *Storyteller's Sourcebook: A Subject, Title, and Motif Index to Folklore Collections for Children.* Detroit: Neil-Schuman/ Gale Research, 1992.

Manning-Sanders, Ruth. *A Book of Dwarfs.* New York: Dutton, 1963.

Massignon, Geneviéve. *Folktales of France.* Trans. by Jacqueline Hyland. Chicago: University of Chicago Press, 1968.

Mayer, Fanny Hagin. *Ancient Tales in Modern Japan: An Anthology of Japanese Folk Tales.* Bloomington, Ind.: Indiana University Press, 1984.

Mehdevi, Anne Sinclair. *Persian Folk and Fairy Tales.* New York: Knopf, 1970.

Olcott, Frances. *The Wonder Garden.* Houghton Mifflin, 1919.

Richardson, Frederick. *Great Children's Stories.* Northbrook, Ill.: Hubbard, 1972.

Sauvageau, Juan. *Stories That Must Not Die.* Edinburg, Tex.: Pan American, 1989.

Sawyer, Ruth. *The Long Christmas.* New York: Viking, 1941.

Sierra, Judy. *The Oryx Multicultural Series: Cinderella.* Phoenix, Ariz.: Oryx Press, 1992.

Skinner, Charles M. *Myths and Legends of Flowers, Trees, Fruits, and Plants in All Ages and in All Climes.* Philadelphia: J. B. Lippincott, 1911, 1925.

Skurzynski, Gloria. *The Magic Pumpkin.* New York: Four Winds, 1971.

Stevens, E. S. *Folk-Tales of Iraq*. New York: Benjamin Blom, 1931.

Thompson, Stith. *Motif-Index of Folk-Literature*. Bloomington, Ind.: Indiana University Press, 1956.

Tichy, Jaroslav. *Persian Fairy Tales*. Retold by Jane Carruth. London: Hamlyn, 1970.

Wiggin, Kate Douglas. *The Fairy Ring*. Garden City, New York: Doubleday, 1967.

Wyndham, Robert. *Tales the People Tell in China*. Illus. by Jay Yang. New York: Messner, 1971.

Zemach, Harve. *Nail Soup*. Illus. by Margot Zemach. Chicago: Follett, 1964.

APPENDIX

AUDIENCE PARTICIPATION FOLKTALES

STORIES WITH IMPROVISATION SLOTS

SUGGESTED GRADE LEVELS FOR TELLING

Preschool

Primary

All stores in this book are recommended for primary-grade telling

Upper Elementary

INDEX

217